LOST IN HANKS HOLLOW

HANKS HOLLOW SERIES BOOK THREE

RACHELLE KAMPEN

PROLOGUE

Dreams of falling weren't much different from falling in real life. Organs felt like they were in a juggling act. Breathing was out of the question. The urge to scream was overwhelming, but no sound emerged.

Rosie Hart had her fair share of dream free-falls. She always woke up with a sharp inhalation, flailing her limbs. The empty air she'd desperately grasped at in her dream was replaced by rumpled sheets she held in a white-knuckled grip, like she was clinging to life itself.

This time was different. This time, it was real. Rosie was falling. She couldn't breathe. She couldn't think about anything but that nothing—no one—was there to catch her.

Then suddenly, she wasn't falling anymore.

Her back met the familiar, scratchy bark of the oak tree. Not just any oak tree. She would know her old oak friend anywhere. Its energy enveloped her like a warm hug, reassuring her that everything would be okay. Her hyperventilating eased, and she pulled in the abundance of oxygen her starved lungs craved. She fisted her hands into the lacy material of the unfamiliar white dress she wore, closed her eyes, and leaned her head back against the trunk. Was it all a dream? It came back to her in flashes, like lightning.

They had been out in wolf form, under a full moon. She and Lucas got separated. Lucas went down. He was wounded. Hunters... guns... her father's eyes staring lifelessly up to the sky.

"Daddy!" The scream exploded from her throat.

"It's all right, Rosie." Her father's voice cut through her panic, and suddenly, he was there. The setting sun behind him formed a halo over his head, like an angel's.

She jumped to her feet then lunged at him, wrapped her arms around his middle, and pressed her cheek to his chest. "Oh, God. Dad, I thought you were dead. It was awful."

"I'm here, Rosie." One of his large hands rested on her head, patting her gently. He wrapped his other arm around her and squeezed her in a firm embrace. Peace fell over her, and she closed her eyes, soaking in his comfort.

"It must have been a nightmare." Rosie's words were muffled as she squished her face into her father's chest. "It felt so real. I was so scared."

"I'll always be with you, Rosie."

The words sounded so final, and her father's energy touched Rosie's senses in a way it never had before. He wasn't the same. Still her father but different. Rosie pulled away, alarm bells ringing in her head.

"What do you mean? Dad? It was a nightmare, right? You're not dead. You're right here with me."

"I'll always be with you, Rosie."

"Stop saying that! Of course you will. You're here with me now!" Rosie took a step back and eyed her father warily. "Right? This isn't a dream, right? You're not really dead. It was all a nightmare. It was just a nightmare."

Rosie's gaze drifted down to the white dress she wore. She didn't own a white dress. What was happening?

A soft smile stretched across her father's lips as tears formed in his eyes. In all her sixteen years, Rosie had never seen her father cry. Not once. He cupped her cheek, and she leaned into the touch, kissing his palm and closing her eyes.

"Rest now, Rosie. Everything will be okay." Slowly, the warmth of her father's hand diminished, and a cold breeze touched her cheek.

Tightness formed in her chest, and she sobbed as she opened her eyes. Dead leaves decorated an empty forest floor where her father had stood only a moment ago. Her legs lost their strength, and she collapsed to her knees. "No. No, no, no."

~

Distant barking spurred a growing dull pain in Samuel Hart's head. The irritation made him restless, and a wave of nausea overcame him. He dug his nails into the couch cushions as a low growl rumbled in his throat. Damn mutts. Probably pissing on all the trees. When the sheriff had promised to bring out the entire police force to scour the woods behind Hart House for Simon's killer, he failed to mention he'd bring the damn search dogs.

On the other side of the living room, Amos's eyes glowed yellow as his lip curled.

Typically, dogs shied away from their property, so the territorial twinges running through Sam's body were something he hadn't experienced before.

Just a cherry on top of this spectacularly horrid night.

"You need to decide, Samuel." Amos's own discomfort over the invasion of their territory colored his tone with contempt and impatience.

The hair on Sam's arms rose. Damn him. If Sam would just get over himself and say yes, Amos would have no choice but to back off. Permanently.

But he couldn't bring himself to answer. The grief was still too near. Too debilitating. The thought of taking over as alpha was the furthest thing from Sam's mind. Besides, what was he supposed to do? Drop out of high school? He couldn't run the pack. He couldn't.

"Come on, Sam. Step up. You know this is what your father wanted."

The desperation in Michael's voice irritated Sam to no end. Michael knew as well as anyone that Sam wasn't ready. But no one wanted the alternative.

The plan had been set in place two years ago. Every alpha had to choose their successor, and his father had chosen Sam to be the future alpha. At the time, Sam had been fifteen years old, so the United States Werewolf Council demanded a contingency plan should anything ever happen to Simon before Sam was ready to take over. At first, Simon had named his cousin Jack as the next in line if Sam was too young, but when Jack was murdered by a member of one of the neighboring werewolf packs months later, Simon had to choose again.

Sam's best friend, Lucas Beckett, and Lucas's father, Roger, were official members of the pack, but they weren't members of the Hart family. They had joined years ago after Roger challenged the Beckett pack alpha and lost. As outsiders, they couldn't be alphas of the Hart pack.

Simon's uncle Stuart was ancient. Out of the question.

That left Simon's cousin Amos and Jack's two children, Daniel and Michael.

Daniel didn't have it in him to be an alpha. Everyone loved him for his soft-spoken, easygoing nature, but he would never be a leader.

Michael had the strength and the backbone, but he also had a short temper. One of the most important duties of the alpha was keeping the peace with the neighboring packs. Michael couldn't do that. His hatred for the Cramer pack was too strong. The moment they all learned Bruce Cramer had killed Jack, only Simon's level head kept the pack from seeking retribution. For Michael and Daniel, the hatred and need for vengeance was much more personal. Jack was their father. Simon had to order a seething Michael to stand down and stay away from the Cramers. Michael still couldn't be trusted around them.

That left Amos, the conceited, self-righteous prick no one liked. It wasn't ideal, but what were the odds that something would happen to Simon before Sam was ready to take over? Better than they thought, apparently.

Now Sam needed to decide whether he was ready to accept the role of alpha or let Amos take over in his place.

"We must inform the Council of Simon's death." Amos took a deep breath, and the yellow glow in his eyes diminished. "You must decide, Sam. You. No one else."

Squeezing his eyes shut, Sam wished to all things

holy this night was all just a nightmare. That hours ago, his father hadn't been killed by a hunter. What he wouldn't give to tell everyone to go to hell while he went to the hospital to make sure the two most important people in his life were all right. Last they'd heard from Roger, Lucas would be okay. The bullet had gone clean through his arm, and he would recover in a few days.

Rosie's life hung on the edge of a cliff, like the one she'd fallen from last night. Sam had made the call to her grandmother, Clara, and she beat the pack to the hospital, impatiently pacing the waiting room with her arms crossed over her large chest. The small room, already cluttered with more chairs than there was space, quickly became overrun with several tense, angry men and one stubbornly stoic old woman. When Sheriff Craig Hill stopped and told them he wanted to start a search of their property, they had to head back to Hart House. Roger stayed behind with Lucas, and Clara promised to keep them updated on Rosie's condition.

What they'd told Sheriff Hill wasn't all that far from the truth. Of course, they couldn't tell him the entire family transformed into werewolves at the full moon and had been mistaken for regular wolves. Instead, they told him that Simon, Lucas, and Rosie had heard gunshots in the woods on their property and went to investigate. The family came upon their bodies later. Lucas told the sheriff it was hunters, but he didn't see their faces. He said they must have been mistaken in the dark for wildlife. Simon and Lucas had been shot, and Rosie somehow fell off the edge of the cliff.

Closing his eyes, Sam breathed through the revolt in his stomach as the images of his father's dead body and Rosie's broken form played over in his head for the hundredth time.

A loud rap on the door made Sam's heart leap into his throat. Everyone else jumped to their feet. All eyes turned to Sam. For now, he was alpha. It was all up to him. Keeping his head high, he moved through the living room to the foyer and took a deep breath as he opened the front door. The sheriff stood on the porch, his red-rimmed eyes staring back at Sam. He and Sam's father had been close, and he hadn't taken the news of Simon's death well.

"Can I come in, Sam?"

"Of course." Sam moved aside as the sheriff stepped over the threshold. "Come in and take a seat."

Sheriff Hill nodded as he moved into the living room and sat on one of the large leather sofas. "We found a hunter."

The tension in the room thickened as the sheriff took a breath. "Ballistics still needs to confirm by matching the bullet pulled from your father with his gun, but he was found on your land, so it seems pretty certain."

"Who was it?" Sam's fingernails dug into his palms as he clenched his fists. Lucas hadn't seen the person who shot him. Who knew what Rosie may have seen.

Sheriff Hill met Sam's stare, sorrow forming pools in his eyes. "We found the trail of a few hunters, but we only found Paul Lewis."

Sam turned away from the sheriff, hiding his eyes, which were probably glowing yellow. The rumble in his chest was too low for the sheriff to hear. Paul Lewis. The local hunter who had been a thorn in his father's side for years. The man with a vile piece-of-shit son who'd tried to force himself on Rosie at a party last spring. The man his father had argued with over and over. He breathed through the rage. He couldn't shift. Not here. Not now.

Sam lifted his gaze to what was left of the pack. Michael, Daniel, Stuart, and Amos watched him warily. They contained their anger much better than he could. Some alpha he was.

"He's dead, Sam." Sheriff Hill's voice cut through Sam's rage, and he fought the urge to look at him. He didn't trust himself. Not yet. "He was mauled by a wild animal. Damn fool. Probably a wolf."

A wolf? No one from the pack had killed Paul. A wolf wouldn't dare set foot on their territory. What the hell was going on? *In through the nose. Out through the mouth.* Sam tried his damnedest to curb his anger, but he could feel the change starting. He had to get out. "Excuse me, please."

He rushed from the room and hurried down the hall, through the dining room, and out the patio door. Outside, officers and hounds still littered the yard, and Sam fought the urge to scream. Whirling around, he made a dash for the cook's kitchen, leaped over the small wooden table, and tore open the door to the basement. Taking the stairs two at a time, he barely made it to the cold concrete floor before his body exploded forward, shifting into wolf form. The urge to howl was maddening, but he managed to stifle it with a whimper as he hurried into the back room with the old prison cells. He scampered into one of the cells and curled up in the corner, hiding his head beneath his tail like the coward he was.

When footsteps on the stairs roused Sam from his haze of rage and despair, he looked up to find Amos and Michael standing in the doorway. Sam curled his lip and growled at Amos's smirk as Michael's stare of pity burned into Sam's conscience. His disappointment was as palpable as Amos's elation.

Shifting to human form, Sam lowered his head as his cheeks heated. He felt like he was eight years old again.

"I'm sorry. I can't do it. I can't be alpha."

ONE

SAM

"Let's see. Bill Kline caught a big-ass walleye last week. Set a record for the biggest fish caught on Mingan Lake, like, ever." Sam propped his feet up on the bed and leaned back in his chair. He tipped his head up toward the ceiling as he thought.

"Oh! And the diner is getting a new owner. I caught a glimpse of her the other day. She's hot as hell. A little older than my usual taste, but I would definitely overlook that fact for a piece of that—" Sam glanced at his sister. "You know what? I can feel you swatting my leg and telling me to grow up, and I don't appreciate it. *You* grow up."

The click-whoosh of the respirator was his only reply. Rosie had always been stubborn. He studied her face. Though she hadn't had sun in a year and a half, freckles still dotted her pale skin. She would look like she was sleeping peacefully if it weren't for the ugly tube taped to her mouth. Her red hair splayed out over the white pillow like trails of blood. His stomach churned, and he closed his eyes.

"Lucas is graduating Saturday. Barely. His grades suck. Surprised? Yeah. Join the club. He's supposed to be the boy genius." Sam clenched his teeth. He typically tried to avoid talking about Lucas in his sister's presence, but something spurred him forward. "I know he hasn't come by. Don't be too mad at him for that, okay? I was at first. I was furious. I kept bugging him to come with me to see you, but he never would. God, I was pissed. But then I saw him crying in his room one day. Something in his face... I don't know. I left him alone about it after that. I mean, don't get me wrong. We've all bawled over you, Rosie—" Sam paused and looked at his sister. "Don't let that go to your head. Once you're out of here, we'll all go back to pushing you around like the little brat you are."

A sigh escaped as Sam placed his feet on the ground and reached forward to touch his sister. The warmth of her skin reassured him, and he ran his fingers over the back of her hand. "Don't tell Lucas I told you about that. He'd kill me. He loves you. Like really loves you. I think I always kind of knew that, but the way he's been... kind of cemented it, you know? He wouldn't even come out of his room most of the summer after you fell. He never talks anymore. Never smiles.

"Jeez, I'm a downer, aren't I? I came here to cheer you up. I just wish I could think of something to say that was cheerful. Truth is things just kind of suck. Amos is an awful alpha. Surprise, surprise.

"I know, I know. You're disappointed in me. I should have stepped up. I know that, okay? Believe me. I know how badly I screwed up."

"Stop beating yourself up, kid."

At the sound of the voice, Sam leaped to his feet and spun. "Jesus, Clara. Warn a guy."

Rosie's grandmother chuckled as she moved into the room and sat on the small sofa in the corner. Taking a sip of her tea, she eyed Sam over the top of her cup with that annoying all-knowing look she always gave him. "You know Rosie would never blame you for turning down alpha, Sam. You were a child."

Sam lowered his head. They'd had this conversation a dozen times. Clara was the only person outside the pack house who knew about their werewolf double life. The woman had kept the secret since she learned about them the day her daughter gave birth to Rosie. With a werewolf father and a witch mother, Rosie was the only female werewolf in existence. When Rosie's mother died shortly after Rosie was born, Simon made the decision to keep in close contact with Clara. He knew nothing about the witch magic that his infant daughter had inherited, and they would need Clara's wisdom in the years to come.

Though Simon had gotten the Council's approval to let Rosie live among the pack, he never told them about Clara or about Rosie's witch heritage. Sam lived in fear that Amos would out them now that he was alpha, but so far, he'd kept quiet about it. Thank God, because if the Council found out, Rosie's grandma might end up a midnight snack, and Sam didn't know if he could keep the Council from pulling the plug on his sister.

He would never admit it out loud, but sometimes, it was nice to talk to Clara. She had that whole freaky witchy-magic-empathy thing that Rosie had. She was always at Rosie's bedside, so Sam quickly learned that if he wanted to visit his sister, he would have to get used to Clara's company.

Most of the time, Clara sat next to Rosie, holding her hand tightly. Clara would squeeze her eyes shut in concentration, and a frustrated sigh would escape after a few moments. Sam knew what she was doing. He had only seen Rosie use her healing magic twice, but he knew Clara healed people on a regular basis. Her healing witch powers were secret, so she sold healing ointments, oils, and candles and pretended they were what healed her customers. The fact that she couldn't heal her granddaughter was destroying her.

It was destroying Sam too. The doctors said Rosie would never wake up, but every time Clara tried her healing mojo, Sam couldn't help feeling a tiny bit of hope. And every single time it didn't work, the disappointment was just as crushing.

"I'd better head out." Sam touched Rosie's hand one last time before he leaned down to kiss her forehead. He stood and faced Clara. "Roger and I are going over this summer's rental contracts this afternoon... then tonight is a full moon."

"Rosie would be so proud of you, Sam. You've come a long way over the past year."

If anyone else had said it, he would have scoffed. But the words were so genuine coming from Clara that he could only bask in the praise and feel reassured.

"Thank you, Clara. That means a lot." A grin twitched at the corner of his mouth. "Especially coming from a man-hater such as yourself."

Clara's jaw dropped. If she had been closer, she would probably have smacked his knee. "I don't hate *all* men."

"Oh. So it's just werewolves then."

"Just the chauvinistic assholes who think they rule the world. If it just so happens that description fits most werewolves...well, there you have it."

∼

Sam stood at the edge of the cliff, staring up at the full moon. In the distance, Amos called to him with a long, impatient howl. Sam had wandered off too far from the pack, but he felt the pull to come here. He sat back and howled in response, letting Amos know where he was. That wouldn't be enough for Amos, though. Sam had to get back. Amos wasn't a patient man, and he definitely wasn't a patient alpha.

If only Sam had paid more attention to his father and taken his training seriously, they wouldn't be stuck with Amos leading the pack. It was a mistake that haunted him, and he tried making up for it by studying harder, like Simon had always wanted. Roger had taken over teaching him the family business. Sam knew they owned a lot of property in the touristy small town of Hanks Hollow, but he'd had no idea how much went into managing the real estate. All the talk about finances and tax laws had Sam's head spinning at first, but he caught on to it pretty quickly.

Amos wasn't good at business or people, so Sam also took over handling the political end of things with the humans. He befriended the sheriff, attended the city council meetings, and cultivated a relationship with the chamber of commerce. He attended as many social activities as he could, becoming well known in town. One of the things his father had always drilled into him was the importance of maintaining a social presence in town to preserve their privacy. It always sounded backward to Sam, but he quickly learned that the best way to keep people at arm's length was to give them a social facade to hold on to. They weren't as likely to spread rumors about the strange family who lived in the woods when he stood right in front of them, delighting them with so-cial grace and pouring money into the community.

Along with local politics, Sam tried to keep on top of things in the werewolf world, though Amos was reluctant to let him in on too much. Amos liked to tout his power in the pack by calling all the shots. One of the first things he'd done as the new alpha was cancel the arrangements Simon had made with the Legacy Agency, where a surrogate was waiting to carry Michael's child. Instead, Amos announced he would father a child himself when the time was right. Amos despised the idea of using the secret agency in Canada, which lined up surrogate mothers to carry werewolf offspring. Since there was no way Amos would risk losing his place as alpha by leaving the pack for a year to go to the city and find some name-less homeless woman to mother his child so that he could steal it away after it was born, Sam worried his intention was to resort to the old method of impris-oning a woman in their basement. A shiver ran up Sam's spine. The old, outdated practice was frowned upon by the Council, but they didn't forbid it. The idea of Amos getting some poor woman pregnant then locking her up until she gave birth was bad enough. What came after...

Sam shivered again. He had no intention of eating anyone.

Still, Amos's pride kept him from arranging for someone else to father a child instead. As a result, there were no immediate plans for growing the pack.

After another impatient howl from Amos, Sam turned and headed back toward the pack, knowing he was about to get his ass handed to him. As he ap-proached, Sam wasn't surprised to find Amos pacing impatiently while the others lay around, looking bored.

With his hackles raised, Amos flashed his teeth in fury. *"Where the hell have you been?"*

Sam was used to hearing his pack members in his head. Their telepathic conversations sounded no different from a vocal conversation. Thank God, they couldn't hear each other's thoughts—only the words they projected.

"I got lost." He didn't bother trying to make the lie sound convincing.

Amos snarled as he approached Sam. *"I'm tired of your attitude, pup,"*

"I'm sorry," Sam lied. *"It won't happen again."*

Behind Amos, Michael let out a long yawn, his tongue stretching out over sharp white teeth. This scenario played on repeat—it was old news. Daniel lay on the ground next to him, his fluffy coat covered in a layer of dirt, as though he'd just been rolling around. Roger groomed himself next to a tree, and beside him, Lucas looked to be sleeping. Stuart had stayed back at the house. He had changed with the full moon, but he remained in the yard, his old body too frail to join the pack on a run.

Amos let out another snarl.

"Everyone back to the house." A low growl accompanied the command.

"Finally," Michael muttered as he and Daniel stood and headed back toward the house.

Roger nudged his son. As Lucas roused, he yawned and stretched his front legs out in front of him before the two of them trotted back.

"Don't forget who is alpha, Samuel," Amos said as he turned and followed the others.

If Sam could roll his eyes in wolf form, he would have.

Just to piss Amos off, Sam took his time returning to the house. As he passed by what was left of Rosie's favorite spot at the edge of the woods, he dipped his head. A memory flashed through his mind of his sister sitting by the roots of her oak tree, her back leaned against the bark as she talked to the wildlife around her.

Crossing through the large yard, he breathed in the smell of the blossoming trees. The flowers in the garden didn't bloom the same way they once had. Despite Daniel's top-notch groundskeeping skills, they all knew nothing would truly flourish again.

Not without Rosie.

The other pack members headed inside, already dressed, as he approached the sprawling patio behind the enormous house where they all lived. Only Lucas remained. His overgrown wavy mop hid his face as he tied his shoes.

"Hey, Lucas," Sam called after he shifted to human form. He reached for his jeans and pulled them on, hopping on his toes as he shimmied them over his butt and zipped the fly. "Ready for graduation?"

Not looking up from his shoes, Lucas shrugged. "I guess."

"Kind of a big deal, right?"

"Not really." Lucas shrugged again.

"Yeah, I guess. I wasn't all that psyched when I graduated either." A year older than Lucas and Rosie, Sam had graduated the year before.

Lucas finally looked up, and Sam flinched. A ghostly pallor replaced the previously glowing complexion, and dark circles hung beneath dull eyes. The light of intelligent, sarcastic humor was gone. Clothes hung loosely over thin, malnourished limbs. Sam shouldn't have been surprised. This wasn't a new look for Lucas. Still, it hurt to see it.

"Hey, I was thinking about heading to Miller's. Want to join me?" Sam knew how Lucas would respond, but he had to try.

"I don't think so. Thanks, Sam." Lucas got up from his chair and headed toward the house.

"Lucas. Please. I could use a friend." Sam was playing dirty. He was fine. But it was the only way Lucas would say yes. His friend had retreated into himself, but he wasn't an asshole. He would be there for Sam when he needed him.

Lucas stopped in his tracks and turned a wary glance toward Sam. "Everything okay?"

"Yeah. I just need to get out of this house, you know? Amos..." Sam shrugged. It wasn't entirely a lie.

"Yeah." Lucas nodded. "Okay."

TWO
BECCA

Tapping her pencil against her notepad, Rebecca Miller fought the urge to roll her eyes. The Beckinsales sat at the same table every Friday night. Still, Mrs. Beckinsale seemed to find it necessary to scour the menu at a snail's pace, as though anything had changed in it for the past five years.

It's all the same damn food that was there last week!

Becca gave her biggest smile. "Are we ready to order, or do we need another minute?"

Mrs. Beckinsale didn't look up from the menu. She ran a chubby, wrinkled, manicured finger over the choices. "What comes with the cod dinner?"

Becca fought the urge to scream. God! That's what she ordered last week. Becca pointed at the menu as she read off the side choices. "Choice of potato and soup or salad."

"Hm. I think I need another minute."

"For cryin' out loud, Agnes. Just order something." Mr. Beckinsale crossed his arms as he craned his neck back to stare up at the ceiling.

"Oh, all right, then, Lenny. Jeez." Mrs. Beckinsale looked at Becca. "I'll have the cod."

"Great! And what kind of potato?"

"What kinds of potatoes are there?"

Deep breath. "Fries, mashed, and baked."

"No hash browns?"

"Only at breakfast."

"Oh dear." Mrs. Beckinsale's large shoulders slumped under her purple Sunday dress. "I was hoping for hash browns."

"I'll see if the cook will warm some up for you."

"Oh. Are they frozen hash browns?"

"I believe so."

"Oh." Mrs. Beckinsale wrinkled her nose and picked the menu up again, pursing thin lips painted with pink lipstick. The thick smell of talcum powder and perfume wafted around her. "Never mind, then. I guess I'll have a baked potato."

"Okay." Becca wrote the order down and prepared herself for the next question. "And will that be soup or salad?"

"What kind of soup do you have?"

"Baked potato soup."

"Well... I'm getting a baked potato as my side, so baked potato soup seems like overkill." Her shoulders shook as she laughed.

Becca tried to make her own giggle sound genuine.

"What kind of salad do you have?"

"Garden or Caesar." Becca kept her voice light and friendly.

"What comes on a garden salad?"

"Carrots, onions, cucumbers, and croutons."

"No lettuce?" Mrs. Beckinsale laughed again, and Becca giggled in response.

"Oh, of course there's lettuce!" Becca put her hands out. "You're too funny, Mrs. Beckinsale!"

"That sounds good, dear. And I'll take my dressing on the side."

"Great! What kind of dressing?"

"What kind do you—"

"Ranch, Italian, French, Thousand Island, or bleu cheese."

"Ranch, please."

"Sounds great!" Counting to ten under her breath, Becca took the menus and headed toward the bar, where her father was busy with one of the taps.

"Hey, sweetie." A smile crept onto her father's face as Becca approached. "Mrs. Beckinsale being a pain again?"

The elderly couple always stayed for hours, exchanging gossip with the other locals. Friday-night fish fry at Miller's was akin to fellowship at the local church. The women gossiped while the men exchanged hunting and fishing stories. Always the same people, the same stories.

Becca slumped against the bar and stuck her lip out as she eyed her father. Short and stout, with a mop of thick gray hair, large glasses, and an ever-present smile, Charlie Miller was everyone's friend. Hours out on the water left a glowing tan on his skin, and he always wore a polo shirt tucked into khaki slacks. "What are you doing behind the bar? Did David call in sick again?"

"Yep."

Her father's restaurant had the best food in town. The only real competition was the diner, but it didn't have the supper-club feel people craved when they headed to Northern Wisconsin. During tourism season, a crowd gathered every evening, but their busiest night was always Friday. Miller's Friday-night fish fry was legendary.

"What is it this time? Strep again?"

"Something like that." Charlie glanced at her and raised an eyebrow. "You'd better get the Beckinsales' order in before she changes her mind."

Becca laughed as she jumped up and headed to the computer kiosk to punch in the order. After finishing, she scanned the dining room and spotted Wendy, the new hostess, toward the back, seating another table in Becca's section. She groaned in frustration before noticing who was being seated. Lucas Beckett's messy brown mop towered over everyone else in the restaurant. Man, that kid was a skyscraper. Next to him, only slightly shorter, Sam Hart's golden curls were unmistakable. They each took a seat in the corner booth as Wendy handed them their menus.

Becca's mind immediately went to Rosie, and she swallowed the lump that formed in her throat. The lifelong hardcore crush she'd had on Sam didn't end the day she heard what happened to her best friend, but she tried her hardest to ignore it. It seemed wrong to lust over her best friend's brother while she was in a coma.

Still, she couldn't help the flutter in her chest when she saw him.

Reaching up to her hair, she sighed at the mess that touched her fingers. She darted to the bathroom then quickly combed her fingers through her long blond tresses, trying to fix her sloppy mess of a ponytail. At least her makeup was on point.

After making herself look as neat as she could, she jogged back out to the dining room and took a deep breath as she approached the table where Lucas and Sam sat. They said nothing to each other as they examined the menus, and it struck her as sad. They had always been so close. Now they looked like strangers.

"Hi, guys." Becca flashed a giant smile as they each looked up at her.

"Becca! How are you?" Sam's genuine smile weakened her knees, and she immediately got lost in his auburn eyes. The legendary trait that all the Harts shared were like pools of cherry chocolate.

"I'm all right! It's Friday night, so you know. Busy." She shrugged and glanced at Lucas. Sad eyes. No smile. That was Lucas now. It made her want to cry. "Are you ready for graduation, Lucas?"

He shrugged petulantly, and irritation colored his tone as he mumbled, "I guess." He jerked then reached for his knee. "Ow! What was that for?"

Becca's gaze swung to Sam just in time to catch his cheeks redden before he covered his face.

"Sorry, Becca. Lucas seems to have forgotten how to behave in public. You know... because he doesn't go anywhere. Ever." Though Sam spoke to Becca, he stared daggers at Lucas.

"Dude, if I knew I was in for a lecture, I wouldn't have come." Lucas sighed and glanced at Becca. "I'm ready for graduation, Becca. Are you?" Without waiting for her answer, he turned back to Sam. "Happy?"

"Ecstatic." Sam scowled.

"Great." Lucas turned his stare back to the menu.

"So... um, do you guys want something to drink?" Her dry mouth made it difficult to speak. "Or are you ready to order?"

"I'll take a Little Lumberjack Stout." Lucas didn't look at Becca as he placed the order.

"Don't be an ass, Lucas. You know she can't get you beer." Sam kicked Lucas again.

"Ow! Quit doing that, asshole! It's a nonalcoholic beer."

"Doesn't matter," Becca said. "We don't have it."

"Fine. I'll take a cola."

"Make it two, Becca. Thank you." Sam's smile weakened her knees a second time.

Smiling back, she turned on her heel and headed toward the bar.

"Hey, Dad, do we have any nonalcoholic beer?"

Her father laughed as he wiped down some glasses. "This is Wisconsin, Becca. Everyone is an alcoholic. Any nonalcoholic beer we carry better have a long shelf life."

"Well, we just had a request for some. And actually, I've heard a few similar requests from the tourists. They're asking for the fancy craft stuff. We better start branching out."

"Yeah, I don't have time to learn about all that stuff. You know that, Bec."

"I know."

Her father worked hard. Maybe she could learn a little about it for him. It would probably involve reading a lot of boring crap, though. "Table eleven wants two colas."

Charlie reached for a couple of glasses and filled them with ice before pouring cola into each as he glanced at table eleven. His face brightened. "Is that Sam?"

Becca tried to hide her grin. Charlie had been close with Sam's father, and he took it hard when his friend died. Simon used to come into the bar quite a bit to eat lunch or dinner. Charlie often sat down with him, and the two of them spent hours talking. Over the past six months or so, Sam had started doing the same thing, and her father seemed to really love having a piece of Simon back in his life.

"Yeah. It's Sam and Lucas."

"Lucas? Lucas Beckett?"

Becca nodded.

"His dad used to come in here every once in a while. Smart man."

"Apple didn't fall far from the tree." Becca frowned.

She took the sodas from her father and headed back toward table eleven. "Here we go, boys."

And then it happened. As she reached forward to hand Sam his soda, Wendy bumped into her from behind. The next few seconds played in horrid slow motion as her hand jerked forward, spilling the full glass of soda directly into Sam's lap. He jumped in his seat, his hands shooting out and smacking Lucas's soda out of Becca's other hand. The glass tipped forward, spilling cola and ice over the top of Sam's head.

"Holy shit!"

Becca turned to Lucas before a huge smile spread across his face, and he roared with laughter.

Horrified, she turned back at a soaking-wet Sam.

Sam glared at Lucas as he flicked ice cubes out of his hair and wiped soda from his face. "You think that's funny, you little shit?" He whipped an ice cube at a still-laughing Lucas, and it hit Lucas in the forehead.

"Oh my God. Sam, I'm so sorry!" Cursing at her shaking hands, she grabbed a handful of napkins and started wiping soda from his face. "I can't believe I did that. I'm so sorry."

"It's okay, Becca. It was an accident." An amused smile lit Sam's face as he stared across the table. Glancing up at Becca, his smile widened.

What was he smiling at? She looked across the table at Lucas, and it dawned on her. Lucas was still laughing—hard. How long since he'd shown any kind of emotion?

Though her cheeks were still flame hot with embarrassment, relief coursed through her as she looked back at Sam's triumphant grin.

Rosie stomped through dead leaves and pine needles, her bare feet catching on sticks and debris that cut painfully into her skin. She'd been walking forever. These woods were as familiar as the back of her hand, yet she found herself walking in circles. She couldn't get out. She couldn't get home.

Cold bit at her fingers and toes, and she hugged her arms around her body. The temperature was pleasantly warm, yet her limbs felt like ice. Inside, the glowing embers of her mate bond barely touched her. The roaring fire that once warmed her heart had died down. She craved its heat. *His* heat.

Every cell in her body ached for him. She longed to run her fingers through his hair and feel his touch against her skin. Was he okay? Was he hurt? Not knowing tore a giant hole through her.

She sighed as she came across her oak for what felt like the tenth time that day. Gently placing her palm against the trunk, she rested her forehead against the bark and fought tears.

Her father's words came back to her. *Just rest, Rosie. Everything will be all right.*

Rest. It sounded good. She slid to the ground and

leaned against the oak. Her eyelids became heavy, and she closed them. She curled up into the enormous roots that stretched along the forest floor like arms ready to cradle her to sleep. Her breath evened out, and the images came before she knew she was sleeping.

It wasn't the first time she'd had the bizarre dream. It was the same every time. The clouds parted, and a golden ray of sun stretched across the sky and down to the earth, like a giant glowing slide. Next, a chariot emerged, led by a pack of wolves. Driving the chariot was a large, bearded man with long, thick, curly hair. Antlers stood prominently atop his head. Fur covered his muscular arms. The bottom half of his body was deer-like, complete with hooves and a tail.

Next to him, a woman more beautiful than anyone Rosie had ever seen stretched her arm out of the chariot like a kid reaching out of a car window to feel the wind through her fingers. A crown of flowers sat on long, beautiful tresses that wisped in the wind. Blossoms formed at her fingertips and trailed behind the chariot in a flurry of colorful petals.

That was it. The dream never went any further.

But this time...it did.

Suddenly, she was standing in the forest, the beautiful woman and the stag-man before her. The woman wore a white gown embroidered with flowers, not unlike the gown Rosie wore. The stag-man carried a bow and arrow. Their eyes bored into her, and her heart raced with fear. She wanted to run, but her feet stayed frozen to the earth.

"Don't be afraid, Rose." The woman's angelic voice echoed like a choir.

It took a full minute before Rosie could speak. It was barely a whisper. "Who... Who are you?"

"We go by many names. What we are called is not important." The woman moved forward, and a small smile stretched across her face. "We're here because of you, Rose."

"Me?"

The stag-man's low, powerful voice vibrated the earth beneath her feet. "You harness the gifts of both the God and the Goddess."

Her grandmother's voice suddenly filled her head, and her breath hitched at the memory of the words she'd spoken to Rosie.

The God selected men from the earliest tribes and blessed them with the power to transform into the ultimate hunters. As wolves, the Chosen men could hear and see and smell better than any creature. They provided food and protection for their people.

The Goddess picked women from the earliest tribes and blessed them with powerful energy that allowed them to commune and become one with the energy of everything around them. The Chosen women brought peace and healing to the people of the tribe, and they helped things grow.

"You're them. You're the gods." Her heart thundered in her ears. The dream was taking a bizarre turn. "What do you want with me?"

The Goddess stepped forward again. Her voice was like music, but her words terrified Rosie to her core. "The Chosen have strayed. You are meant to bring them back together."

Rosie looked around. They had to be talking about someone else, but there was no one else there. She swallowed before putting a hand to her chest. "Me?"

A small smile on the Goddess's cherry lips was the only response.

Shaking her head emphatically, Rosie took a step back. "I'm not...I mean, I can't."

"It's why you're here, child." The ground rumbled again as the God spoke.

"No." Rosie shook her head again. "No. I just want to go home."

"You can't go home yet, Rose," the Goddess said. "It isn't safe for you there."

"What do you mean, 'it isn't safe'? What about my family? What about Lucas?"

"You're the link. The Chosen children belong together. If the wolves change their ways, the witches will come."

"But what..."

The Goddess's gaze trailed over Rosie's shoulder. She turned to see what she was looking at, and her stomach somersaulted in excitement.

"Lucas!" Tears of joy sprang to her eyes as she took a step toward the base of the oak, where he was sitting. The flames of her mate bond roared to life, warming her limbs.

But just as quickly as they burst forth, the flames burned down to smoldering embers. His name died on her lips, and she stopped in her tracks as she studied his face. A single tear trailed down his cheek.

"Lucas?" She whispered his name again, but he didn't look at her. "What's wrong with him?"

Rosie turned toward the God and the Goddess, anger vibrating through her body, but they were gone. She took a step toward where she'd seen them a moment ago. What the hell? Turning back toward the tree again, dread pulled her to the ground, and a sob escaped.

Lucas was gone too.

~

When Rosie woke from her dream, tears dampened her cheeks. She looked around. Still curled up in the oak's roots. Still wearing the white dress.

Still lost in the woods.

It had been a dream, right? Of course it was a dream. It had to be. But if it was a dream, did that mean she was awake now? Because things still didn't feel right.

The sound of feet crunching through leaves startled her, and she snapped her head up to find her father standing in front of her again. Her heart skipped a beat, and she leaped to her feet, throwing herself into his arms.

"You're back." Her voice shook.

"I told you I would always be with you."

"I had the weirdest dream." Rosie took a step back to look into her father's face. "And I can't get home. I keep walking, and I just can't get home."

"It's not safe for you there yet." Her father scowled. "You can't go home until Sam makes things right."

Shaking her head, Rosie tried to keep the tears away.

"Don't worry." Simon touched Rosie's chin. "Sam's got it under control. I have faith in him."

"The gods…They told me it wasn't safe to go home in my dream. They weren't real, though, right?" Rosie ran a hand through her hair. Breathing became more difficult. "Dad, that couldn't have been real."

"Relax." Her dad pushed her down to sit on a tree root then sat down next to her. "Just relax, Rosie."

"How can I relax?" Rosie shook her head. "What's happening?"

"It will all become clear with time." He pulled her to his side.

She rested her head on his shoulder, just like she'd done dozens of times before.

"Everything will be okay."

It was a beautiful day for a ceremony. In the middle of the football field at Hanks Hollow High stood the commencement stage. Graduates sat in chairs arranged in a semicircle facing the front of the stage, and the spectators—parents, grandparents, family, and friends—were in the stands, cheering on the students as they crossed the stage to accept their diplomas.

Some kid Sam didn't really know had babbled his way through the valedictorian speech. Lucas should have been up there.

Sam jumped to his feet as they called Lucas's name, and he cheered as his best friend walked across the stage. Lucas didn't smile. He shook the principal's hand, accepted his diploma, and continued without a flicker of emotion.

Sam glanced at Roger. The lines on his face had deepened over the last year, his worry for his son aging him quickly. He clapped, and his thin lips stretched in a smile of pride, but his eyes told Sam he was worried, just as Sam was, that Lucas would never quite be the same again.

Sam's heart ached when the names announced

went from Haas to Hebl. Hart should have been in there. He looked over at Michael and Daniel, and he knew they were thinking it too. The lighthearted humor was missing from Michael's eyes as he looked on with a stony expression. Beside him, Daniel stared at the ground with a frown. Stuart's age was catching up with him, and he hadn't been able to make the trip, but if he had, he would be mourning with them.

Sam listened for one other name, and when he heard it, he stood and cheered, as he knew Rosie would want him to. Rebecca Miller smiled and waved at the crowd as she walked across the stage to accept her diploma. Her eyes were red rimmed, and tear tracks cut through the makeup on her cheeks. The wind picked up, and her long blond hair blew across her face. As she pushed it out of the way, her gradua-tion gown flapped open, and her dress fluttered up, exposing her leg to the upper half of her thigh. Sam raised an eyebrow. She was a knockout, no doubt about it. A little more curvaceous than most of the girls her age, with a prominent chest and hips and a butt that always drew his attention.

His cheeks heated as his mind went there. Shaking his head, he glanced around as though wor-ried someone was reading his thoughts.

As gorgeous as she was, she wasn't Sam's type. She always struck him as shallow and ditzy.

Although...

The other night at Miller's, he'd seen a side of her he hadn't before. After she dumped two glasses of soda all over him, they'd shared a little moment as they watched Lucas laugh for the first time in God knew how long. Something in her smile told Sam she'd known how great that laugh was to hear.

A flurry of graduation caps flying into the air

pulled Sam's attention back to the ceremony. He stood with the crowd and cheered. The last of the pack had graduated. They were all adults now. A brief wave of nostalgia pulled at him, and he fought off the sting of tears as his mind went to childhood memories with Lucas and Rosie. He closed his eyes. Don't go there. Not now.

He shook it off as they made their way down toward the field with the rest of the families and fought through the crowd to find Lucas. The class only had fifty-five graduates, and Lucas towered over them all, so it didn't take long.

Roger gave Lucas a firm handshake and a hug. "I'm proud of you, son," he said as he clapped him on the back.

Lucas's mouth twitched in something resembling a smile.

"About time you blew this popsicle stand." Sam gave Lucas a quick hug.

"Yeah, well, I guess I had to leave eventually."

Lucas's bored expression suddenly turned stormy, and Sam followed his line of sight to Mason Lewis. Mason's suave, overconfident swagger from a couple of years ago had been replaced with a stiff posture and a glint in his eye that spoke volumes of his anger at the world. His reputation had never recovered after his father killed Simon. News of what happened shook the entire Hanks Hollow community. The sheriff finally got Mason to confess that he'd been there that night. He'd been hunting wolves with his father and their hunting buddy. He said his father sent him away when they heard voices. The third hunter was never found.

Where the mystery hunter in the orange beanie cap and sunglasses had disappeared to had kept the town buzzing for weeks. Who was he? Where did he go? Mason claimed not to know anything about him.

The pack had been on guard for months. Something in the forest had killed Paul Lewis that night. Mason insisted it was a wolf. It seemed like a wolf attack, but a real wolf wouldn't dare step foot anywhere near Hart territory, and the pack would have smelled a trespassing werewolf from another pack. Bear attacks were almost unheard of. A cougar? Not knowing had nagged at Sam for the longest time.

Simon's funeral had drawn a big crowd. His years of serving on the village board, pouring money into the community, and volunteering around town had earned him a good name with a lot of people. Whispers still flew around town that Paul had been harboring a grudge against Simon for the restraining order he'd filed against him, and Simon's death hadn't been merely the result of a hunting accident. Of course, the pack knew that Paul couldn't have known he was shooting at werewolves and not merely wolves, but they did nothing to stop the rumors.

After all that, things went downhill for Mason. His grades dropped, and he lost his place on the football team. Sam had run into him a couple of times at the gas station at the edge of town, where he worked as an attendant. Doubtful he was headed to college with crummy grades and no sports scholarships to pay his way.

Boo-hoo. Sam couldn't feel sorry for him. He deserved what he got.

Sam felt a tiny poke in the middle of his back and turned to find Becca staring up at him. Tears misted her eyes when she smiled.

"Congratulations, Becca," Sam said, giving her a quick hug.

"Are you going to see her after this?" she asked. Tears still glistened in her eyes, and Sam wondered how long she could hold them there before they spilled.

"For a little bit." Sam nodded. "Then I'm going back to the house to celebrate with Lucas."

She looked over at Lucas, and Sam followed her gaze. He scowled at the ground, kicking at the dirt with his shoe as he absentmindedly twirled his graduation cap in his hands.

"That should be fun," she deadpanned.

Sam stifled a laugh. "You're welcome to join us." It was dumb of him to invite her. The pack would most likely be going for a run. But he had a feeling she would decline his offer anyway.

"I have a thing at my father's restaurant," she said. "Thank you though."

Sam smiled and turned to walk away, but he stopped when she spoke up again.

"But if you don't mind, I'll tag along if you're going to go see her right now."

FIVE

SAM

"You should have been there today, Rosie." Becca held Rosie's hand as she spoke. Tears spilled down her cheeks. "It's always been you and me. R and R. I could really use some R and R time with you."

She closed her eyes as more tears dripped onto her graduation gown. Her shoulders shook with sobs, and Sam reached out to touch her back. She leaned into him, burying her face in his chest. Guilt gnawed at him for his earlier berating thoughts. She wasn't shallow. Not at all. How many times had she been there for Rosie over the years?

He studied his sister's face. He missed her so much.

Becca gave Rosie's hand one last squeeze and moved away, making room for Sam. He leaned down and kissed Rosie's forehead. The smell of antiseptic soap hit his nostrils, and he squeezed his eyes shut, willing away the tears he could feel coming.

The door clicked open, and Sam turned, expecting to see a nurse. Instead, Calvin Cramer stood in the room, eyes round.

"I'm sorry. I didn't know anyone was here." He

swallowed convulsively, and Sam could smell his fear. "I can come back."

"It's okay." Sam sighed. "We were just leaving."

Sam had inspected the list of Rosie's visitors each week over the past year. He knew Calvin had come to see Rosie several times. The first time Sam had seen Calvin's name, his first instinct had been to tell the nursing staff not to let him in the next time he came to visit. But he knew his sister wouldn't want that. For some reason, she seemed to like the weirdo.

Sam winced. Calling Calvin a weirdo wasn't fair. From what Rosie had said, he had it rough. Who was Sam to judge how he dealt with it? How many people taunted Rosie for being strange? Maybe that was part of why she seemed to like him so much.

Calvin studied the floor, doing some strange fidget maneuver with his fingers. He looked up at Sam for a moment, but when he caught Sam staring at him, his cheeks reddened, and his gaze went straight back to the floor.

Sam nudged Becca's elbow. "Let's go."

Calvin moved farther into the room, giving Sam and Becca a wide berth as they headed toward the door. He kept his head tilted toward the floor like a scolded dog.

"Who was that?" Becca whispered when they stepped into the hallway.

"Just a friend from out of town," Sam said. "Rosie likes him, but I think he's creepy."

"I think I'm going to have to go with you on that one," Becca said. "Yeesh."

They walked the rest of the way to Sam's SUV in silence. It was only after they'd climbed into the vehicle that Sam finally spoke up. "Thank you, Becca.

For coming to see her today. You've always been a good friend to Rosie."

Becca nodded. "Oh, sure. Of course." Her face quickly morphed from an easy smile to a mask of sorrow. She squeezed her eyes shut, and tears streamed down her cheeks. Her nod turned into a rough shake of her head. She covered her face and sobbed. "I used to visit her twice a week. Then it was once a week. Then I just stopped. I'm an awful friend, Sam. I stopped coming."

"Hey. Don't do that." Sam reached a hand out, let it hover over her leg for a moment, then snatched it back to his side. He knew what she was feeling. God, how he knew it. He tried so hard to come and see Rosie as often as he could. Guilt gnawed at him. "I used to visit her every day. Now I only make it once a week. You know she would understand."

"She would." Becca nodded as she sobbed. "I miss her so much."

Sam breathed through the sting of tears as he started the SUV and made the silent drive back to Hanks Hollow.

THE MYRIAD of smells that traveled up Sam's nose as he parked the SUV in the garage next to Hart House made his stomach growl in anticipation. Martha had been working all morning to prepare a feast to celebrate Lucas's graduation. As he crossed the giant veranda and stepped into the house, the smell intensified, and his stomach rumbled again. He made his way down the hall to the dining room, where the pack members were seated around the table.

"There he is!" Michael rushed forward and

trapped Sam in a headlock, rubbing his hard knuckles into the top of his head. He reeked of booze. "'Bout time you got home. Now we can get this party started." He dropped his voice to a loud whisper. "No surprise, the guest of honor is kind of being a killjoy."

Sam pushed Michael away and stole a glance at Lucas. Seated at the head of the table, he slouched in his chair with arms crossed, wearing a frustrated scowl. Sam frowned.

"Did you guys leave any food for me?" He clapped his hands together as he looked over the spread on the table.

"There's plenty to eat, dear." Martha made her way into the dining room from the main kitchen and put down a fresh plate of rolls. "Did you go see Rosie? How does she look?"

Sam gave Martha a one-armed hug. "The same."

Martha frowned. "Poor dear. We should be celebrating her today too."

A solemn silence filled the room before Lucas stood and wordlessly stomped down the hall to the staircase. Moments later, Martha flinched at the sound of his bedroom door slamming.

"Darn it. I should have kept my fat trap shut."

"It's not your fault, Martha." Sam patted her back. "He'll be fine."

"That conversation I had with her..." Stuart's soft voice shook, and everyone stilled.

"Grandpa?" Daniel moved to the chair next to his grandfather and placed a hand on the frail man's back.

Stuart looked at Sam. "One of the last times we spoke, I told her about your grandmother."

"My grandmother?" Sam scrunched his face in confusion as he took a seat across from his great-uncle.

"She was the last woman our pack imprisoned downstairs." Age had taken its toll on Stuart's voice, making it tremble so much that he was hard to understand. "Rosie wanted to know if it was true. If I took part in the ceremony that followed the birth of your father. The ceremony when the pack devoured her."

A knot formed in Sam's stomach. Suddenly, the feast on the table didn't seem so appetizing.

"Great dinnertime conversation, Grandpa," Michael groused with a frown. He took another swig of his pilsner before he moved down the hall toward the rec room. "Way to liven up the party!"

The permanent frown that accompanied Stuart's old, worn, wrinkled face deepened. "I didn't want to tell her it was true. I was ashamed. We didn't speak much again after that. Not really." Tears pooled in red-rimmed eyes that stood out prominently over sagging skin. "I'm sorry, Sam."

"There's nothing to be sorry for, old man." Amos appeared as if from nowhere. Clothes pressed, hair combed to the side. He was a dark-haired Jeffrey Dahmer. So creepy. "That's the way the pack operated for hundreds of years. There's no shame in that. It's much better than the test-tube babies Simon tried to push on us."

Clenching his teeth, Sam fought the urge to tell Amos to go to hell. As he looked around the room, all eyes turned in his direction, and Sam swallowed the lump in his throat.

They all expected him to speak up.

His jaw dropped, but the words wouldn't come. Speaking up would lead to a fight. A fight could lead to a challenge. He didn't want to challenge Amos. Not just because he wasn't so sure he could beat him in a fight but because he wasn't so sure he *wanted* to beat him in a fight. As much as he hated how Amos ran the pack, Sam couldn't bring himself to step up and take over.

Sam clamped his mouth shut and rose from his chair. He didn't have Rosie's empathy, but he sure could feel the disappointment in the air. As he retreated toward the stairs and the safety of his room, he said softly over his shoulder, "I'm not so hungry."

SIX

BECCA

Muffled music from inside the bar mingled with the sound of speedboats skimming the water. Below the boardwalk, where stone steps led into the lake, Becca sat and let the small lapping waves splash over her bare toes. With one hand, she fisted her blue dress to keep it dry, and with her other hand, she twisted her hair on top of her head and let the late-afternoon sun warm her shoulders.

"I thought I might find you here. Ditching your own party?"

Smiling at the sound of her father's voice as he descended the stairs behind her, she shook her head. "It's a great party, Dad. Thank you. I just wanted to soak in a little of the sun before it goes to sleep."

"Remember when we used to sit out here and watch the sun set every night?" Charlie nudged her shoulder as his voice took on a nostalgic quality. "It was the best part of my day."

Becca closed her eyes and smiled at the memory. "Why don't we ever do that anymore?"

Charlie sighed sadly. "Too busy. You usually take the evening shifts, and I'm always filling in for whoever decides to call in sick or pull a no-show."

"Hm." Becca nodded. "Business has been good."

"It has. And I can't tell you how much I appreciate you staying on to help your old man instead of going off to college. But I wish you would reconsider."

"Daddy, I told you. There's plenty of time for that. I'm not in any big hurry to leave Hanks Hollow. Eventually, I might go take some business classes or something, but you know I've never really been excited about the whole college thing." She nudged her father's knee with her elbow. "I can learn a lot more about life and business from my old man."

"You really like working here? You're not just saying that because you want to make me happy?"

"I really like it, Dad. You know me. I like to be around people, and I like Hanks Hollow. This is the best place for me."

"Well, then." Charlie sighed and looked out at the water before he slid his gaze back to Becca. "I have to give you your graduation present."

Touching the diamond necklace around her neck, Becca furrowed her brow. "Daddy, you already—"

"That was your mother's necklace. She would have wanted you to have it. Your graduation present is above the bar."

"Above the bar?"

Charlie held out his hand. "Come on."

With a small smile, Becca took her father's hand and stood. She grabbed her sandals and carried them with her as he led her up the stone steps to the boardwalk. They crossed the wood-planked walkway to the large picture window with Miller's Bar & Grill etched in gold letters across the front. Next to the window, a door led to the second-story space above the bar.

Charlie fished in his pocket and pulled out a key

that he used to unlock the door. He held his hand out. "Ladies first."

Smirking, Becca stepped inside. A narrow staircase led to the second floor, where another door led to the upstairs area. She'd only been up there once or twice. Her father used it for storage. After climbing the stairs, she paused before opening the door at the top. As she stepped inside, her jaw dropped.

Gone was the clutter that littered the space when she'd last seen it. Now, a neat living area lay before her, complete with a couch, a chair, and a television mounted to the wall. Becca walked through the living room and spotted a small kitchen to the right and a bedroom to the left. It was a nice little apartment.

"Dad, this must have been so much work!"

"I fixed it up during the day while you were at school." Charlie stuffed his hands into his pockets as he smiled proudly.

"Are you going to rent it out?"

"In a way, yes. It will be the living quarters for my new assistant manager."

Becca's eyes widened. "You hired an assistant manager?" Charlie had never had anyone in a management position before. He had a few shift supervisors, but he handled all the management himself, and it ran him ragged.

Charlie handed her the key. "Becca, you're my new assistant manager."

"*What?*" Becca shrieked. "Shut up!"

"Only if you want to be. The second you decide you want to go to college—"

Becca threw herself into her father's arms and squeezed, jumping up and down on the balls of her feet. "I love it, Dad!"

"Well. It wasn't just for you. I've been wanting to

turn your bedroom into a gym for years. I need to get rid of this gut." He patted his stomach to emphasize his point. "Maybe if I get into shape, the ladies will start knockin' on my door."

"Oh, God. Dad, please stop." Becca clamped her hands over her ears while her father laughed. She looked at him carefully before examining the key, turning it over in her hands. "You're sure about this? You won't be lonely in that house all by yourself?"

"Heck no."

"Should I be insulted by how fast you answered?"

"Ha! Yeah. Maybe."

Charlie laughed as Becca punched him in the arm.

"In all seriousness, Rebecca. You've been adulting for a long time. It's time for you to get a chance to reap some of the rewards for your hard work."

Tears sprang to her eyes as she threw herself into her father's arms again. "Thank you, Dad."

"Oh! I love this song!" Becca turned up the volume on her phone and danced through her old bedroom. Most of her stuff had already been hauled out. Her father helped her disassemble her bed earlier in the morning, and the rest had been fairly simple to move on her own. Her clothes were the biggest challenge. At first, she folded them and put them in boxes. After she filled one box and barely made a dent in her closet, she started leaving them on their hangers and hauling them down to her car, one handful at a time. Her little Volkswagen Bug didn't hold much, so she'd made four trips to the new apartment already.

All she had left was tidying the room. Cleaning

and music went hand-in-hand, so she'd spent the last hour alternating between dusting and dancing.

Lifting her arm, she took a deep breath in through her nose. "Phew!" The short shorts and little white tank she'd chosen for moving day were filthy with dirt and sweat. June heat reared its ugly head outside, a humid eighty-seven degrees. The shower called her name, but the last of her clothes were already stuffed into the back seat of her car, and she would only get sweaty again as she unpacked at her new place.

After tightening her ponytail higher up on her head, she ran the back of her hand across her forehead then put away the cleaning supplies before she headed out to the car.

Driving with the windows rolled down, Becca blasted the radio on the short drive to her new place. She was on cloud nine as she pictured how she planned to decorate her apartment. Visions of brightly painted walls and lots of candles danced in her head as she parked on the street behind her father's restaurant and grabbed a box.

Making her way through the alley toward the boardwalk, she realized she didn't have much to drink in her new place, and she wanted something a little sweeter than water. She decided to stop at the restaurant to grab some lemonade. It wasn't until she got a few odd stares as she stepped inside that she remembered how awful she looked. She shook it off. Who cares?

She spotted her dad sitting at the end of the bar, chatting it up with someone. "Dad, do you mind if I grab some lemonade from the cooler?" She set her box on a stool then made her way behind the bar.

"Yeah, honey. Go ahead."

"Thanks."

She grabbed two bottles and paused a moment to let the cold air brush over her hot skin before closing the door. Then she opened one of the lemonades and took a big drink, nearly shooting it out her nose as she finally spotted who her father was talking to.

Sam Hart's eyebrow rose as he looked her up and down. His gaze lingered on her chest for a moment, and he blushed as his eyes snapped to her face. He cleared his throat. "Um. Hi, Becca."

Hiding her embarrassment as best she could, she flashed a giant smile. "Hi, Sam."

"Are you moving?" His brow wrinkled in confusion.

God, he was so freaking gorgeous.

"Um, yeah. I'm moving into the apartment upstairs."

"Sam, meet my new assistant manager. She'll be living right upstairs so she can be at my *Becca* call."

Charlie laughed at his own joke, and Becca rolled her eyes.

"As long as your beck and call leaves me at least a little room for a social life."

Sam nodded. "Congratulations, Becca."

"Congratulations for what?" Lucas made his way to the bar from the back of the restaurant and sat down next to Sam. He must have been in the bathroom.

Sam turned to him. "Becca is the new assistant manager, and she's moving upstairs."

Lucas nodded, but he stayed silent.

"Do you need help?" Sam stood and moved to the box Becca had placed on the stool. "Lucas and I can give you a hand."

Heat rushed to her cheeks. The help would be great, but she really didn't want Sam to smell her. It was embarrassing enough that he'd seen her all sweaty and gross. "Um..."

"That's really nice of you, Sam, but I want to talk to Lucas for a bit longer. I want to hear more about all this craft beer knowledge he has. Where did you learn all this stuff, Lucas?"

Lucas dipped his head bashfully. "My dad used to help run the brewery where we lived. Beckett's Beer is pretty well known in Wisconsin."

"Huh. That so?" Charlie turned to Sam. "Why don't you help Becca while I talk to Lucas."

Sam glanced at Becca. "Sounds great!"

Charlie beamed. "Thank you, Sam!"

"You bet, Charlie." Sam lifted the box like the weight was nothing. "Lead the way, Becca."

Becca screwed the cap back on the lemonade. "Are you sure?" She prayed the box he carried would stay shut. She was pretty sure it was full of underwear and tampons.

Sam nodded, and Becca moved out from behind the bar. Sam followed her outside, and she fished the key out of her pocket, unlocking the door to her new place.

"I really appreciate this, Sam. It will save me a few trips to and from the car."

"Hey, you're saving me. Once you get Lucas talking about something he likes, it's hard to shut him up." When Becca raised an eyebrow skeptically, Sam laughed. "Hard to believe, I know, but it's true."

"What gets him talking? Wish I had known this years ago. It would have saved me from some long stretches of awkward silence."

Becca made her way up the stairs, and Sam trailed behind her.

"There are two things—music and beer. In that

order." Sam laughed. "Unfortunately, his taste in music is weird. He likes that indie crap. And his knowledge of beer goes into way more detail than most people want to know. So... I actually recommend the long stretches of awkward silence."

Becca laughed. "Good to know." As they reached the top of the stairs, Becca opened the door to her new place.

Behind her, Sam let out a low whistle. "Nice! I would love a space like this."

Becca turned to him and narrowed her eyes. "Don't you live in, like... a mansion?" She pointed at the sofa. "You can just put the box there."

After Sam had done so, he wandered around the apartment, taking it in. "It's a huge house, yes. But a big house means nothing when it's shared with six other people. Sometimes, I just need some alone time, you know?"

Becca pursed her lips. "I guess. But to be honest, I'm a people person. I spent a lot of time by myself growing up. My dad worked late nights at the bar, and I was home alone. It got lonely." She shrugged. "I guess that's why I tried so hard to make friends at school. I never wanted to be alone when I didn't have to be." She offered Sam the unopened lemonade.

He met her eyes for a moment before he took it from her. "You and Rosie are so different. I have to be honest. I never understood—"

"Why we were friends?" Becca laughed. "No one did. I don't know if Rosie and I ever really understood. We're nothing alike. But... I don't know. We just clicked. From the moment I met her, I wanted to be around her all the time. She was like the sister I never had." Becca swallowed, fighting tears. One escaped and trailed down her cheek, and she wiped at it in frustration. "Dammit. Sorry."

Sam's smile widened, and she did a double take when she saw the tears welling in his eyes. "Don't be sorry, Becca."

Their eyes met, and she fell into the depths of deep color. Her heart swelled as he held her stare.

After what felt like an eternity, her lungs begged for air, and she realized she was holding her breath. She averted her eyes, and her cheeks heated. "So. If you're sure you don't mind helping, I'll show you where my car is."

Sam cleared his throat. "I know your little VW. You and Rosie had a lot of joy rides in that thing."

Memories rushed over her. "Yeah. We did."

"Give me your keys. I can haul your stuff up while you start putting things away."

Becca's jaw dropped. "Are you sure?"

Sam gave a little laugh. "Definitely. Smells like you could use a break."

Heat spread up Becca's neck and into her cheeks as she fished her car keys out of her pocket and handed them over. "Is it that bad?"

"You could definitely use a shower."

After grabbing the last of Becca's mounds of clothes from her little VW, Sam shut and locked the car door behind him and headed up to her apartment. He had no idea where she planned to put all of it. The woman had more clothes than everyone in Hart House combined.

As he entered the apartment, the sound of running water met his ears. Guess she finally decided to take a shower. Chuckling, he made his way through the living area and into the bedroom. He laid the clothing on her bed and looked around. She'd made some progress getting things put away, but the room still looked like it had fallen victim to a tornado.

Deciding to help, he grabbed the nearest box and opened it. Heat rushed to his cheeks as his gaze ran over the girly things inside. Tampons and... lots of lace and silk. He glanced toward the bathroom. No sign of her.

He reached for one of the tiny lacy panties and held them up.

Damn. He really needed to start dating again.

"What the hell? Sam!"

His heart leaping to his throat, he dropped the

panties and spun to face a scarlet-faced Becca. Her wet hair spilled over her shoulders, and a fuzzy pink towel wrapped around her. Sam's gaze went straight to her bare legs.

"Seriously?" She pulled the towel around her a little more tightly.

Unable to resist, he laughed. "I just thought I would help you unpack. Grabbed the first box I saw." He snorted. "I'm sorry."

"Yeah, you sound sorry." Becca scowled. "Out! Go unpack in the kitchen!"

Sam was still laughing as Becca shoved him out the bedroom door. He made his way to the kitchen and searched for something to unpack. Not finding any boxes, he moved to the living room and looked through a few there. All were filled with girly knick-knacks, candles, and pictures.

"Becca," he called, "you don't have any kitchen stuff."

The door to her bedroom opened, and Becca emerged, dressed in a pink tank top and jean shorts. Her still-wet hair twisted in tangles over her shoulders. "Oh, right. Yeah, I suppose I'll need to do something about that."

"Do you have anything besides decorations and lacy underwear? I can go unpack those for you if you want."

Sam smirked as Becca picked up a handful of packing peanuts and threw them his way.

"You know, I always thought Rosie exaggerated, but she didn't. You're horrible!" She threw another handful of peanuts.

Laughing, Sam batted her hand away and jumped out of reach. "Okay, okay. Truce. What can I do to help?"

"Don't you need to go rescue Lucas from my dad?"

"Lucas and I drove separately. He can leave anytime he wants." Sam shrugged. "I can stay and help you."

Something flickered across Becca's face before her cheeks flushed. "Oh. Okay. Thank you, Sam." She tucked her hair behind her ear and smiled shyly. "I guess there isn't that much more to do other than unpack the boxes in here." Becca raised her hand as Sam started to speak. "I will take care of what's in my bedroom, thank you very much."

Sam shrugged. "If you say so."

He situated himself on the floor and started unpacking picture frames, knickknacks, and candles from the nearest box while Becca disappeared into the bedroom.

Half an hour later, boxes emptied, Sam looked around for something more to do. As his gaze drifted across the room, he spotted a framed picture of Rosie and Becca. He picked it up and sat down on the sofa as he examined it. The photo had been taken on a boat. With their arms around each other, both girls wore huge grins. Rosie looked happy. Really happy.

"That was taken the summer before her accident."

Sam looked up as Becca drifted into the room.

"It was a great day. We took the pontoon out on the lake for a few hours. We had so much fun. Rosie got burned, of course."

"Of course." Sam smiled as Becca sat next to him on the sofa. "She was always getting sunburned. She loved the sun, but it didn't really love her."

Becca ran her finger over Rosie's image. "That was the first time I finally got her to wear a bikini. If it were up to her, she'd go swimming in a wetsuit and scuba gear."

Sam laughed. "That would be okay with me."

"I'm sure it would." Becca rolled her eyes before sliding her gaze over to Sam.

The blue of her eyes popped against her tanned skin. She radiated a warmth and intelligence Sam had never noticed before. Maybe he just hadn't been looking. His eyes trailed down to her full pink lips. He leaned forward and tilted his head slightly before reason took over, and he pulled away.

This was Becca. Rosie's best friend. What was he doing? "I better head home."

Frown lines formed on Becca's forehead, and her cheeks pinkened. "Yeah, I guess I better get things organized around here."

They both stood, and Sam made his way to the door.

"Thank you so much for your help, Sam." Becca shyly tucked her hair behind her ear again. "It was really nice of you."

Sam smiled. "Rosie would kick my ass if I didn't help her best friend."

Another frown formed, and Becca nodded. "I'll see you around, Sam."

EIGHT

SAM

Whistling a tune he was only mildly familiar with, Sam had a small skip in his step as he made his way down the hall for breakfast. Truth was he couldn't stop thinking about Becca.

He couldn't have been more wrong about her. She wasn't the shallow, ditzy type he'd always pegged her for. There was more to her. Part of him—the part that didn't scream at him that it was all kinds of wrong—really wanted to find out how much more there was.

"Someone has a spring in his step this morning." Michael smirked at him as he dug into his eggs.

"He helped a damsel in distress yesterday." Lucas's mouth twitched in a half grin. "A very hot damsel in distress."

"Niiice." Michael laughed. "Sammy got some!"

Sam gritted his teeth and glanced to his left, where Amos sat at the head of the table. The alpha's jaw clenched as his grip tightened on his fork. His face reddened as his lip curled.

Great. Just what he needed—the wrath of Amos. He quickly shifted his attention back to the table, filling his plate with bacon and eggs as he grumbled a warning. "Shove it, Michael. It wasn't like that."

"She shot you down, huh?" Obviously not able to read the room, Michael stuck his lip out in a fake pout and laughed.

"Enough!" Amos's shout wiped the smirk from Michael's face. "It's enough that you all think you can run around town with any girl you please." He paused as his eyes roamed around the table. "Let me make myself clear. There better not be any little whores winding up pregnant with one of your spawn. Don't think for one second I won't rip out her throat. I thought I made myself clear. I will sire the next generation of this pack."

Tense silence lingered in the air. If only it were an idle threat. Truth was, it was real. Amos was crazy enough to do it.

Sam turned his gaze toward the alpha. "It was nothing. I just helped her move. Nothing happened. I swear it."

Feeling the disappointed stares of his pack mates, Sam kept his head low as he finished his breakfast in silence.

"You can't do that, Michael!" Daniel's irritated voice carried through the rec room.

"Funny. I think I just did."

Sighing, Sam turned up the volume on the television, but it only served to make the others raise their voices. It was just the news. He wasn't really paying attention, but anything was better than listening to their bickering.

"You didn't follow suit on the last hand. You're totally cheating." Daniel's face reddened in frustration as he threw his cards onto the table.

Next to Daniel, Lucas rolled his eyes. Minutes earlier, Michael had practically forced Lucas to play with them, as they desperately needed a fourth. Stuart looked ready to fall asleep in his seat next to Michael. His cards drooped forward in his lax grip.

"Forget it," Daniel continued. "I quit."

"Oh, come on! Don't be a baby!" Michael pushed the cards back toward Daniel.

"Come on, guys. Give it a rest!" Roger yelled from the armchair where he'd been quietly reading. "You're acting like a bunch of kids."

"I can't play with him." Daniel got up from the game table and strolled across the rec room toward the couch. He sat down next to Sam and crossed his arms.

Michael stood and stomped toward the hall, smacking the back of Daniel's head and muttering under his breath on his way out of the room. "You're such a pansy."

"That was a waste of time." Lucas got up from the table slowly and mumbled under his breath as he left the room. "I'm going for a run."

The only one left at the card table was Stuart. The old man didn't appear to have noticed that the game was over. After a few moments, he sighed and stood up. Slowly and unsteadily, he made his way over to the couch and sat next to Daniel and Sam.

"Sorry, Grandpa," Daniel mumbled with a frown. "Didn't mean to ruin the game."

Stuart raised his hand. "Your brother is so much like his father." He closed his eyes and smiled. "Jack liked to push people's buttons too. Used to drive me crazy."

Sam turned his attention back to the news. He was about to turn the channel when the anchor caught everyone's attention.

"The debate continues over whether an off-season hunt is warranted on the local wolf population after a series of livestock killings in recent weeks. The DNR has maintained that the wolf population will be endangered by a hunt, but local leaders are insistent that something needs to be done. The DNR says that killing livestock is out of character for wolves..."

A graphic popped up on the screen, showing where livestock killings had occurred recently. Sam's stomach tightened. The killings were heavy in the Becketts' territory in the northeast part of the state. They were also heavy in the Cramers' territory in the northwest. No killings had been reported in the central-Wisconsin Hart territory.

"Well, that doesn't look suspicious at all." Daniel's voice was low. "I'm surprised we haven't heard from the other packs."

"Who says we haven't?" Sam set his jaw. "The other packs could be declaring war, and we would never know it. Amos doesn't tell us anything."

"Is there a problem?"

Amos's low hiss behind Sam sent a jolt through his stomach, and he closed his eyes, muttering a curse.

"If you have something to say about the way I'm running this pack, I'd love to hear it."

Standing, Sam turned to face his alpha. "I apologize, Amos." Sam didn't miss the annoyed glare Daniel cast his way. "I meant no disrespect."

Amos's lip curled, his anger palpable. He took a menacing step forward. If it weren't for the sofa separating them, Sam was sure he would have been shoved to the ground.

"It sounded like disrespect." Amos's gaze flitted to the others in the room. Something flickered across his face. Nervousness? He set his jaw, his eyes turning steely as he returned his stare to Sam. "Don't forget your place, kid." Sam didn't have the chance to respond before Amos spun on his heel and strolled from the room.

The disappointed silence that hung in the air weighed heavily on him.

I'm not the damn alpha.

With a sigh, Sam tossed the remote control onto the sofa cushions and made his way out of the room.

Hours later, Sam hadn't peeked his head out from the confines of his bedroom. He felt like a petulant kid, but he really just wanted to be by himself. When someone knocked on his door, he had to throttle the urge to scream at whoever it was to get lost. His luck, it would be Amos. Who was he kidding? Amos wouldn't knock. He'd just barge in.

"It's open." He didn't move from his spot on his bed, staring up at the ceiling. He continued throwing the ball up toward the ceiling and watching it fall back toward his face before catching it with one hand.

The door creaked open, and Roger stepped inside, closing the door behind him.

"Hey, Roger."

"Sam, I need to talk to you."

"I gathered that." Sam sat up and tossed the baseball to the floor. "What's up?"

Roger stuffed his hands into his pockets and examined the pictures on the wall before he sat next to Sam. "I have a confession to make."

Curiosity piqued, Sam nodded for Roger to continue.

"I never told your father, but I've been talking to my cousin Shawn for years. He's been keeping me updated with news from the Beckett pack."

Sam's jaw dropped. "You kept this from my dad? How could you do that?"

"If I had told him, he would have been forced to tell Marcus. I think he always suspected. It was sort of a don't-ask, don't-tell situation."

Sam nodded. It sounded like something his father would do.

"I heard from Shawn yesterday. Marcus is fed up with Amos. He's been asking for a meeting for months, but Amos has repeatedly refused him."

"Is it about the livestock killings?"

Roger nodded. "They've had a rogue on and off for years. It's started mauling the area livestock and causing a stir with the locals."

It was shitty of Amos to refuse meetings with other packs. Traditionally, the packs had at least one friendly visit each year for the sake of diplomacy.

"There's more." Roger looked hesitant. "Shawn said the rogue smells like your family."

"That's not right." Sam scowled, remembering years ago when the Cramer pack had made the same claim. "We've all been here. No one has left."

"I know," Roger said. "I don't get it either. But Shawn wouldn't lie to me. He's smelled the rogue himself."

It all sounded suspicious. A rogue that smelled like their pack. Livestock mauling that affected the neighboring territories but not the Hart territory. Amos was putting them in some hot water by refusing to meet.

Sam chewed on his bottom lip. "Why are you telling me this, Roger?"

Roger exhaled a long breath. "I can't tell Amos. You know that. I had to tell someone. It had to be you."

"I'm not the alpha."

"But you should be."

"But I'm not." Sam snapped the words out, and Roger flinched. "The sooner the pack gets used to that, the better."

"Sam. Someday, you're going to have to—"

"Please, Roger. Spare me the talk about how I need to do what my father wanted me to do. I failed him. I failed the pack. It's done."

"It's not done. You can challenge him."

Sam huffed out a breath. "I'm not strong enough."

A sad smile spread across Roger's face. "You don't give yourself enough credit, Sam. You never have. Think about how far you've come. You're running this pack already. We all look to you."

Clenching his jaw, Sam averted his gaze.

"Just think about it, kid." Roger patted his knee before he stood and moved to the door. "We all have faith in you. Have a little faith in yourself."

NINE

LUCAS

Frayed edges lined the plain, threadbare black shirt. Nothing special, but she'd always seemed to like it. Always wanted to wear it. Lucas picked it up and turned it over in his hands, as he'd done a dozen times before.

His mate bond smoldered just below the surface, in the back of his mind like a fire that refused to be extinguished. The glowing embers kept the creeping darkness at bay. The heat reminded him how bright the bond burned when they were together.

Someday, she would come back to him. This nightmarish life without her would be done. Though he didn't deserve it, she would forgive him, and things would go back to normal. Until then, he just had to muddle through. But as time stretched on, muddling became harder and harder.

He held the shirt to his face and took a deep breath, inhaling the lavender scent that still lingered. The smell brought forth a pain that seared his skin, but he sucked in another breath then another. The pain was real, and it reminded him of the love that had brought him to this place. He never knew he could hurt this much, but he would do it all again. He would face a lifetime in the fiery pits of hell to have her here with him now.

He stretched the shirt over his pillow and laid his head on top of it then picked up the latest Stephen King thriller, took a deep breath, and began to read. It could almost...*almost*...feel like she lay next to him.

He was fully engrossed in chapter five when the knock came at his door. Huffing an annoyed sigh, he rolled off his bed and tossed the book onto his pillow. As he crossed the floor, he steeled himself, already knowing it was his father there to hound him, as he did most days.

As he opened the door, Roger pushed his way into the room, glancing around before he turned to Lucas and ran his gaze up and down his body before zeroing in on his face.

"Have you eaten today?"

"I'm fine, Dad."

"You didn't answer my question."

"I ate at breakfast."

"No, you didn't," Roger snapped. "I was watching."

"Fine." Lucas sighed and shrugged. "I'll eat a big supper. What's up?"

Roger nodded toward the door and took a seat on Lucas's bed. Lucas shut the door and pulled his desk chair across the floor to sit across from his father. Roger picked Lucas's book up off the pillow and studied it.

"I used to read Stephen King," he said quietly. "You've probably read all his books by now. My favorite was always *Pet Sematary*."

"It's a good one." Lucas nodded and leaned forward, resting his elbows on his knees.

"I haven't heard of this one." Roger examined the book, turning it over. "Is it new?"

Lucas nodded. "I don't think you're here to talk about books. What's going on?"

Roger blew a long, slow breath out through his mouth then stared into Lucas's eyes. "I want you to start coming with me to see the pack again."

Averting his eyes, Lucas clenched his jaw. This again. A few months ago, his father had started bothering him about it. Their monthly meetings with the Becketts had stopped after the attack a year and a half ago. He'd known his father would ask him to start going again eventually, but he just couldn't bring himself to do it. If he went, they would start grooming him to become alpha again. What was the point? The only reason he'd wanted to become alpha in the first place was because the Council had ordered Rosie to mate with one. Now...

"The pack needs you."

Lucas flicked his gaze to Roger's face at his pleading tone, and the desperation in his eyes made a knot form in his stomach.

Still, he had no desire to be alpha. He needed to be here when Rosie came back to him. Then if the Council still wanted her to mate with an alpha, they'd figure it out. If she would forgive him, that is. Until then, he would wait here for her. He shook his head, but before he could speak, Roger raised his voice.

"Son, Shawn is drowning. Between keeping the business going and trying to keep Marcus from making dumb mistakes—"

"I'm not going to be alpha, Dad!" Lucas stood, and the office chair rolled across the floor. "They'll have to find someone else."

"You boys..." Roger stood, his face morphing

quickly from desperation to anger. "You boys and your refusal to accept responsibility. If you don't step up, the future of all werewolves is doomed. You can't be kids forever."

Roger shouldered past Lucas and reached for the door, swung it open, then slammed it shut behind him.

ROGER'S WORDS still dogged Lucas the next day when he decided to venture into town to find something to do. He needed to get away from the silence. If he had to stare at his walls any longer, he'd jump out the window.

He made his way down to the garage to his white F-150. The pack gave the Ford dealership in town good business. Their garage was full of vehicles they'd purchased from the lot. He'd gotten the truck last year after Sam graduated from high school, and Lucas needed a way to get to school. It was nothing special, but it got him around. It blended in with the dozens of others in town just like it, and Lucas was all about keeping a low profile.

After making the short drive into town, he pulled into a spot on Lake Street, facing the park. The day was overcast, but it didn't stop the tourists from shopping along Main and sitting in the park to eat and listen to one of the local bands play corny cover songs.

Old people danced on the small makeshift floor in front of the gazebo stage, and others filled the picnic tables as they ate and listened to the music. Parents sat in the grass while their kids played.

He didn't feel like eating, and the off-tune poor excuse for a band was making his ears bleed. Deciding to head to the boardwalk, he hopped out of his truck, then he crossed Lake Street before making his way through Miller's alley to the lake. He strolled to the edge of the boardwalk and leaned on the railing. The wind painted choppy waves on the water. It looked like it would rain any moment. The normal clutter of boats and jet skis was missing, and the resulting quiet nagged at him. All he had lately was quiet.

Behind him, the low hum of activity from Miller's pulled at him. He turned and headed across the boardwalk and into the bar, and a cacophony of noise hit his ears—idle chatter, laughter, the clang of dishes.

He shoved his hands into his pockets and moved slowly toward the bar. Finding an empty stool, he sat down next to an old man who eyed him up as though he were a punk kid in a country club. He averted his eyes, scanning the area for the bartender.

"Lucas!" Behind him, Charlie Miller strolled across the floor and crossed behind the bar. "Good to see you, kid. I actually wanted to talk to you. Can I get you something?"

"Cola would be great." A small smile twitched at his lips. Charlie had personality. "Thanks."

"You got it," Charlie said as he grabbed a glass. He filled it with ice and moved to the tap, pressing the button for cola. As the fizzy liquid sprayed over the ice, Charlie looked at Lucas. "I've been thinking a lot about our conversation the other day."

"Yeah?" Lucas watched as Charlie placed the cola in front of him.

"Yeah." Charlie rested his hands on the bar. "I could use someone like you around here. How would you like a job?"

TEN

ROSIE

Another dream. It had to be. She still wore that silly white dress. In the distance, a house stood out against a forest that looked different. She didn't recognize some of these trees, but the landmarks, the shape of the area... There was no mistaking it. She was looking at Hart House—or a different version of it.

The rustic structure was uninviting. Dated and old but intimidating nonetheless. It stared down its nose at her. Judging. Willing her away. No room for people like her in this world. Unsightly, disorderly, unruly. The wind hurled the whispered word at her in distaste.

Witch.

From within the house came a scream. Piercing, agonizing. Rosie's heart thumped wildly, and she covered her ears, squeezing her eyes shut tightly.

Just a dream. Just a dream. Just a dream.

The scream pierced the air again, and Rosie's feet carried her forward, toward the towering nightmare made of rotting wood. As she moved closer, a light from the in-ground cellar door drew her in.

That door... Hart House might have changed over

the years, but the cellar remained the same. The same splintered wood cellar door still covered the back entrance to the basement in the Hart House that she knew, though it was rotted and half covered in weeds.

She stumbled forward and peered inside. A small staircase led down to the basement. Fear made her stomach cramp, and she turned to run, but the agony in the scream she heard from the base of the stairs spurred her forward.

Carefully making her way down the staircase, she stared at the cell room of Hart House. She'd played there as a child. As she got older and grew into her powers, she began to feel the traces of terror left in the room from the horrors of the past.

The horrors playing out in front of her now....

A woman knelt on the floor. Blond hair fell in a snarled mess around her shoulders. The red that stained her faded, dirty dress matched the red pooling around her legs. Just outside the cell, the men ignored her cries as they gathered around an infant wrapped in a blanket. Rosie studied them and gasped when she saw a face she recognized. In youth, he looked much different from the wrinkled man she knew. The face, though, was unmistakable.

"Stuart." She whispered the name.

"Please." The woman's cries fell on deaf ears. "Please give him back to me. Please let us go."

Rosie stepped back, her heart in her throat. Terror overpowered her burning desire to speak for the poor woman. Tears burned her eyes as she recognized what she was witnessing. The birth of a werewolf... and that meant that they were about to kill the woman in the cell. Rosie couldn't stand there and watch them eat her. She lunged forward and reached for the bars.

"I'm going to get you out of here."

The woman looked right through her, continuing her litany of pleas with the men.

"Listen, they aren't going to help you. You have to forget about the baby. Come with me. Please."

Frustration clawed at her as she tried and tried to unfasten the bolt. It wouldn't budge. And the woman continued to stare through her.

Rosie turned toward the men. They didn't seem to notice her presence. It occurred to her then. Dream or not, she had no control over the outcome of what happened, as if she didn't exist.

Having no intention of sitting and watching the scene play out, Rosie ran for the stairs. As she reached for the cellar door, it slammed shut with a thunderous bang.

"No. Hell no." Rosie pushed and pushed on the door. It wouldn't budge.

"Take your baby upstairs, Samuel." The voice of one of the men behind Rosie caused her to spin on her heel.

For a moment, Rosie looked for her brother. Then she remembered Sammy had been named after their grandfather, Samuel Hart. Simon's father. A slow, horrible realization dawned on Rosie. If the infant was her father, that meant the woman in the cell was her grandmother.

The woman wailed, reaching her slender arms through the bars of the cell. "No! Please! That's my baby!"

Samuel glanced toward the cell, his face pinched in concern. "Alfred, I thought you said you wouldn't—"

"Take the child upstairs, Samuel." Alfred repeated the command with the authority only an alpha could project.

"Alfred, it's tradition for the father to make the kill and take the first choice of meat," Stuart said.

Rosie winced, and her stomach tightened. Stuart talked about the woman in the same way her pack talked about taking down a deer and arguing over who got first dibs on the parts that tasted best raw.

"Your brother has made his choice, Stuart," Alfred said. He glanced toward the woman then quickly turned away. "I won't force him to take part."

"But—"

"As his brother, you may take his place." Alfred said. He frowned, and his gaze turned to the woman again. For a moment, Rosie thought he might change his mind, but then he straightened and looked at Stuart. "You may make the kill and take first choice of meat."

Stuart's angry scowl morphed into uncertainty as he glanced toward his brother. Samuel turned away, making his way quickly toward the stairs, holding the baby tightly to his chest. When Stuart turned back toward the room, he eyed the woman, and his irises glowed yellow. He moved forward slowly.

The rest of the pack followed, surrounding the cell. The energy in the room shifted as the men channeled their wolves.

The woman scurried to the back of her cell, alarmed at their yellow eyes. "Monsters! What are you?"

Alfred spoke as he opened the cell door. His voice held a note of regret. "We will take good care of the child."

One by one, the men shifted to wolves, and the woman screamed as they converged on her.

"No!" Rosie shrieked as she watched Stuart curl his lips back, flashing his bright-white teeth.

Stuart lunged forward, and Rosie cried out as he bit down on her grandmother's leg. She squeezed her eyes shut and clamped her hands over her ears as shivers coursed through her body. Tears wet her cheeks as she sobbed. "Stop, please! Stop!"

Quiet replaced the growls and screams, and Rosie cautiously, slowly, opened her eyes. The forest lay in front of her. No cells. No wolves. No bloody grandmother. She choked on a relieved sob as the shivers continued to vibrate through her body.

"You've got to be kidding me. There's no way—"

"Sam, it's just a matter of time before Congress approves an off-season hunt on the wolves. We're hearing about livestock killings all over Northern Wisconsin." Lenny Beckinsale leaned forward, making himself heard over the low hum of conversation around them.

Miller's lunch hour drew a crowd today, and Sam couldn't help but notice some of the stares aimed his way as the other customers eavesdropped on their conversation. He should have known what he was walking into when Lenny had asked him to lunch. The man was head of the local hunting club.

"Your family owns most of the land around here. Good hunting land. Everyone loved your father and everything he did for this town, but the one thing that kept him at odds with the locals was his reluctance to allow hunting on his land. Now that you're running things—"

"Nothing has changed." Sam set his jaw. "I'm not going to turn our land into a free-for-all for a bunch of trigger-happy lunatics." He knew that last statement wouldn't win him any friends in a town full of avid hunters, but his patience was wearing thin. "Did you forget what happened the last time we had hunters trespass on our property? My father was killed. Hell, my sister is still in a coma. The answer is no. There will be no hunting on any of the Hart property. Period."

Lenny leaned back and nodded. "I figured as much." His mouth twitched in a smile, but the frustration behind his stare was unmistakable. "Can't blame a guy for trying."

"Fair enough. Can we talk about something else now?" Sam lifted his fork and stabbed the bed of noodles on his plate. "How's the wife?"

"Oh, she's got some new craft hobby that's got her driving to Rhinelander twice a week. I swear that woman isn't happy unless she's spending all my money."

Sam laughed around a mouthful of spaghetti. His gaze drifted around the room and landed on Becca as she leaned down to pick up a dropped piece of silverware from the floor. As she straightened, her long blond hair fell over her back. He wanted to run his fingers through it so badly it almost hurt. Tight jean shorts hugged her curves and showed off her long, smooth, tanned legs.

"She's a looker, ain't she?" Lenny smiled at him. "I ask to be seated in her section every Friday night."

When he realized he'd been caught staring, Sam's cheeks heated with shame. Becca deserved better, and he felt the urge to defend her. "She's a really nice girl. She and my sister were very close."

Lenny's predatory smile dropped. "Yeah. I'm sure she is. Charlie raised her right, I'm sure."

"Smart too. She's helping Charlie manage the restaurant."

"That so?" Lenny glanced in Becca's direction. "Say, what's Lucas doing these days? Now that he's graduated, I'm sure he's off to college."

Clearing his throat, Sam shook his head. "He's taking some time at home, deciding what to do."

"I never understood his relation to your family."

"No relation. Roger was a close friend of my father's." Sam wiped his mouth with his napkin as he rattled off the practiced line that had been drilled into him years ago, though it wasn't that far from the truth. It just left out the part where they had joined the Hart pack because they'd been kicked out of the Beckett pack after Roger challenged the alpha and lost. "He and Lucas moved in when Roger started helping out with the family business."

Lenny crinkled his brow. "Huh. Nice of your father to let them live there with you."

"We have plenty of room. And Roger has been a huge help."

Lenny nodded before he glanced at his phone. "Well, I better head home. Agnes will be wondering where I've gone off to before too long."

"It was good talking to you, Lenny." Sam stood and shook Lenny's hand. "Glad to hear we understand each other."

"Right." Lenny quirked his mouth in a half grin as he held Sam's gaze for a moment before he turned and headed for the door.

"Asshole."

He'd muttered the word, so he jumped in surprise at the response that greeted him.

"He's always been an asshole." Becca slid into the chair across from Sam. "How's the spaghetti?"

Her blue eyes bored into his, and his breath caught in his throat. How had he never noticed how striking they were? "It's great."

"Don't tell my dad I told you, but he uses Ragu."

A laugh shook his shoulders. "The secret is safe with me."

"I don't doubt that. You're a good guy." A genuine smile lit her face. "Thanks again for your help the other day."

"It was no trouble." When it looked like she was about to get up, a pesky jolt of longing overcame him. He didn't want her to leave. "Are you working this afternoon?"

"I just got done."

"I have to check on the rental properties on the other side of the lake. I was going to drive, but it's a gorgeous day. Maybe I'll take the boat." He eyed her carefully. Hoping. "Would you like to join me?"

THE WIND WHIPPED through Sam's hair as the speedboat skimmed over Mingan Lake. He glanced behind him and laughed at the way Becca's long locks flew in every direction. She scowled as she tried to wrangle her hair with her hands.

After two trips around the lake, enjoying the thrill of speeding through the open water, he found a spot near the opposite shore and slowed the boat to a low idle before cutting the engine. He glanced over at Becca as she stretched her body out across the bench seat, soaking up the warm sun. Her little striped bikini hugged her body perfectly, covering just enough to drive his imagination wild.

"This is perfect." Becca closed her eyes. "I've

been dying to go out on the water, but no one ever wants to go. It feels weird to take that big pontoon out by myself."

"I don't go out very often." Sam shrugged. "I don't know why. I always forget how soothing it can be." The water glittered under the afternoon sun, and the soft waves gently rocked the boat back and forth. He let his gaze slide over Becca's body again before he quickly shifted his focus back to the water. "How are things in the new place?"

"Good." Becca sat up and set her elbows on her knees. "It feels strange to not have someone waiting at home for me, though. At first, it was really cool. But then...I don't know. It's kind of lonely. Like, if something happened, and I didn't make it home, no one would know. I don't really like that feeling."

"I never really thought about it like that." What she'd said set him on edge. "That's kind of morbid."

She giggled. "Sorry. Didn't mean to be such a downer." She looked out at the water for a moment before she turned back to him. "What about you? How do you like running the family business?"

"I hated it at first. I spent years dreading it and gave my dad such a hard time about it. He tried so hard to get me to learn." Sam took a deep breath. "But now that I've gotten into the swing of things, I really like it. My dad built something great. I mean, the business has been in our family for generations, but he's developed a good relationship with the town. I wish he was still alive so I could tell him that."

"You're a lot like him. You know that?"

Sam looked away. "I'm not."

"You are. People flock to you, just like they flocked to him. You've got some kind of weird magnetism."

"Magnetism?" Sam cocked his head and raised an eyebrow skeptically.

"Yes, magnetism." Becca laughed. "People like you. My dad loves you, and he's the best judge of character."

"Your dad is awesome."

Becca beamed. "He is, isn't he? He's a good guy. And a great dad."

Not sure if it was a sensitive subject, Sam hesitated before he asked his next question. "How long has he been on his own with you?"

A touch of emotion flickered in Becca's eyes. "My mom died when I was a baby. I don't remember her. It's always been me and my dad, although I have an aunt who visits a lot. She introduced me to makeup and *Vogue* magazine. She was there for all the girly things my dad couldn't handle." Her brow crinkled as she appeared lost in thought. "Rosie told me her mom died when she was born, but she never told me what happened to your mom."

Frowning, Sam debated whether to stick with the typical evasion. Something made him want to tell Becca more. "I never knew her." That was the typical line. "My father never told me much about her."

What was there to tell? His mother had been a surrogate who was paid to carry him for his father. She was nothing. Just some random woman. Sam went through life trying to tell himself he didn't need a mother. He never told anyone how much it hurt to see other kids with their moms and know that somewhere out there, the woman who'd given birth to him was walking around without giving him a second thought.

"I guess mothers are a rare breed around here." Becca's smile didn't meet her eyes.

Sam tried to smile back. She had no idea how right she was. "I guess so." Warmth spread through him, and he averted his eyes. "Becca?"

"Yeah?"

"If it would make you feel any better, you can text me each night when you get home. That way, if you don't make it home, someone will know." He flicked his gaze back up to meet hers.

"Thank you, Sam. That means a lot."

TWELVE

LUCAS

Lucas's feet slapped against the pavement, and he breathed steadily in through his nose and out through his mouth. The fresh scent of pine trees mingled with the smell of his sweat. He kept an even pace as he rounded the curved road that cut through the thick forest.

Slowly, he was working a morning run back into his routine. He woke at sunrise, dressed in sweats, tied his sneakers, and hit the road. It was the only thing that got him out of bed. He loved the rhythmic feel of his feet hitting the ground as the fresh air hit his face.

Not much else kept him occupied lately. He'd been climbing the walls since graduation. Sitting around with nothing to do but think was driving him crazy. Because all he could think about was her. Red curls. Brown eyes. Freckles. A sweet smile.

Blood.

Broken bones.

Her brilliant red hair splayed around her body.

He stopped in the middle of the road and bent over, resting his hands on his knees as he took deep, heaving breaths.

God, Rosie.

Tears leaked from his tightly closed eyes, and he fought the urge to scream. It still felt like only yesterday, yet it also seemed like an eternity.

Any day now. She would be back any day now. She had to be.

He straightened and used his sweatshirt to wipe his face. After taking a quick glance around, he started running again, focusing on the rhythm of his steps. Ahead, the gate that led to Hart House peeked out from the trees. He slowed his pace as he turned up the long driveway. As the house came into view, he slowed to a walk, flipping his hood over his head to soak up some of the sweat that drenched his hair.

"I'll never understand people who run for pleasure."

Pausing, Lucas tilted his head up and shielded his eyes from the sun as he stared up at the source of the voice. Up on a ladder, Michael was cleaning leaves from the gutter over the garage. The muscular man took care of most of the household maintenance.

"Weren't you in wrestling in high school? You have a million trophies in your room."

Michael shook his head. "Nuh-uh. No comparison. Wrestling is way better than running."

"If you say so." Lucas shrugged and started making his way toward the house—back to his room to stare at the wall some more. Pausing, he turned back toward Michael. "Need a hand?"

"Nah." Michael grabbed a handful of wet leaves and tossed them to the ground. "I'm almost done."

Trying not to let his disappointment show, Lucas nodded and jogged up the front steps. As he made his way inside, he spotted Sam in the office, going over some paperwork. He took a deep breath. He'd rehearsed this in his head. It was now or never. He flipped the hood off his head and cleared his throat. "I want to get a job."

Surprise lit Sam's face as he jerked his head up. "What?"

Lucas took a deep breath. "I want to get a job. I can't sit around here, doing nothing."

Sam nodded. "Okay. Okay." He leaned back and studied Lucas. "Do you have something in mind?"

Bracing himself for a fight, Lucas squared his shoulders. "Miller's. Charlie offered me a job."

"As a server?"

"Bussing for now," Lucas said. "And he said I could be backup bartender."

Sam raised an eyebrow. "Bartender? Don't you think Charlie will want someone older?"

"I'm eighteen. I'm old enough to serve. And I know beer. Dad's taught me a lot about craft brews, and Charlie said he likes the idea of someone who knows their way around the industry. Tourists want that kind of stuff. I can help him. I can tell him what to buy. And there's a whole new industry of nonalcoholic craft that's emerging. It will draw in a lot of business from the younger crowd—"

"Okay, Lucas." Sam held up his hand. "I get the picture."

Lucas shuffled his feet and put his hands into his pockets. "I need this, Sam. I need something to keep me busy."

It was unusual for pack members to have jobs outside the pack house. Lucas knew that, but he hoped Sam would let him give it a try.

"You'll have to get permission from Amos."

"Yeah." Lucas kicked at the floor with his sneaker. "I might need your help with that."

A muscle in Sam's jaw twitched. "I'll take care of it. Don't worry."

"Are you sure?"

"Yeah. I can convince him." Sam smiled reassuringly. "Amos is a jerk, but he has a big ego. People with big egos are easy to manipulate. You just have to talk up how great the idea is and make it sound like he thought of it. You'd be surprised how easily he falls for that."

Lucas tried not to let his skepticism show. Amos didn't seem like the type to be easily manipulated. "Thanks, Sam."

IF THERE WAS A GOOD PLACE FOR ROSIE TO BE lost, the forest was it. Even after all this time, she couldn't get sick of it. The trees called to her. She knew them. The chirp and croak and screech of foraging animals brought life to her tired limbs.

All day long, she walked. She inspected the plants, sharing her energy with them. The animals kept her entertained with their antics. Squirrels chased each other. Raccoons fought. Deer cautiously wandered through the trees, nibbling on plants and bark.

When she slept, she had vivid dreams, so much more real than she knew a dream could be. This time, her dreams took her back to Hart House again. Standing in the living room, she watched the roaring fire in the fireplace. Stuart sat in the rocking chair next to it, one of his journals in his lap. He was younger, the Stuart she remembered from her childhood. This could have been any one of a hundred snowy winter evenings.

A young version of her bounced through the room and threw herself into Stuart's lap. Her bright curls danced, matching the fire.

"Read to me, Stuart!" The lisp caused by Rosie's missing front teeth told her she must have been around six. "Please?"

"Hello there, little darling!" Stuart gave a rare genuine smile, one he seemed to reserve only for Rosie. It had always made her feel special. "What have you been up to today?"

As the young version of Rosie recounted her day, Rosie scowled through tears. What she wouldn't give to go back in time and erase the newer images of Stuart that tainted those special memories. No matter from what angle she looked at him now, he wasn't the same. A cold, heartless killer sat in that rocking chair where her warm, loving great-uncle had once sat.

"Don't judge him for the mistakes of his past, Rosie."

Her father's voice startled her, and she looked to her left, where he had suddenly appeared.

"Do you really think the Stuart you're looking at now would do those terrible things he did years ago?"

Rosie swallowed past the lump in her throat. "How can you forgive him? He killed your mother." A tear slipped down her cheek. "I saw it, Dad. I saw it all. He was wild...relentless...evil."

"It was a different time." Simon shook his head. "If it weren't for the alpha who raised me, I would have been isolated from society and brought up to believe that women were to be hunted. That thinking was drilled into Stuart from a young age. He knew nothing but the pack. The only time he saw a woman was behind those cell bars." Simon smiled. "Until you came along."

"What made you decide to keep me?" She couldn't look him in the eye as she asked the question that had haunted her for years. "You knew it was dangerous. Why take that chance?"

"Are you kidding?"

At her father's incredulous laugh, Rosie turned to him.

He stepped toward her and placed a hand on her cheek. "The moment I saw you, I was in love. There was no choice. No question. I would have done whatever it took to make sure you lived." He nodded toward Stuart. "And it didn't take long for the others to follow suit."

Rosie tilted her head. "Not all of them. Amos would have killed me if he could. It's a miracle Stuart didn't, according to what I saw."

"In another time, he would have."

Rosie flinched at her father's words.

"But Stuart learned to love you. And that love grew over the years, more and more. Think about the power in that. For him to go from the ravaging, wild creature you saw... to this."

Across the room, Stuart read to the young Rosie and stroked her hair. She rested her head on Stuart's shoulder as they rocked. Her eyelids began to droop, and Rosie felt the pull of sleep on her own eyes.

"It's time for me to go." Her father put a hand on her shoulder. "You sleep now."

"Don't leave, Dad." Rosie turned to him. "You keep leaving me."

"I'm never leaving you." Simon smiled. "I'm always around. Promise."

THE DEAFENING SILENCE AT THE DINNER TABLE made Lucas dread mealtimes. Gone were the days when conversation was so loud and rambunctious that Lucas couldn't hear himself think. He always thought he hated that. Now he missed it. No one wanted to talk. Not while Amos sat at the table. In the past, when Simon had been alpha, Amos was the one who sat in silence, a disgusted sneer on his face. Now he vocalized his distaste for everyone and everything. It didn't take long for everyone else to learn to hold their tongues.

Lucas rested his head against his hand as he smooshed his potatoes with his fork and watched them flatten. Then he traced mashed potato lines across his plate. He stirred his peas and carrots in to make a mushy mess.

"Lucas."

Straightening, an apology on the tip of his tongue, Lucas looked toward Amos then averted his gaze immediately. "Yes, sir?"

"I hear you got offered a job at Miller's. I want you to take it."

Surprised, Lucas turned to Sam. His friend winked as a victorious grin spread across his face. Lucas couldn't believe it. The freaking genius had done it.

"Yes, sir." Lucas turned his gaze back down to his plate, hiding his smile. He even took a bite of his mashed potato mush.

As the dinner dishes were cleared, Lucas rose from the table, ready to make a beeline for town. His father's hand on his shoulder stopped him. "I need to talk to you, son."

Lucas had never considered his dad wouldn't approve of his getting a job. He figured he'd be elated over Lucas getting out of the house. Maybe he should have talked to him about it first. As he followed his father up the stairs to his bedroom, his stomach tightened. If he had just put Sam through the agonizing task of getting Amos to agree to him getting a job only to have Roger put a stop to it...

"I heard from Shawn today," Roger said quietly as they entered his bedroom. He shut the door behind them. "I need you to listen carefully, Lucas."

Sitting down on his father's bed, Lucas nodded, quietly celebrating the fact that Roger didn't want to talk about the job. "Yeah, Dad. I'm listening."

"Marcus Beckett is in the hospital."

Jaw dropping, Lucas sputtered for a moment. "What happened?"

"He drank himself sick. His son, Brody, found him passed out at their house and couldn't wake him." Roger shook his head. "Shawn said Brody showed up at the pack house, crying for help. Poor kid is only twelve. Too young to have to deal with something like that." He closed his eyes for a moment.

"That's awful." Lucas frowned. He couldn't imagine what the kid must have gone through. Lucas glanced at his father. Roger bit his lip and studied the floor. Lucas knew where the conversation was headed, and his stomach tightened. *Just when things were looking up.* He shook his head. "Dad—"

"Shawn is going to have to take over while Marcus is in the hospital." Roger met Lucas's eyes. "The time is coming. If Marcus doesn't recover, Shawn will have to take his place as alpha, and he's going to want to hand leadership over to you."

"Dad—"

"They need us, Lucas! They need *you.*"

Lucas flinched at the emotion displayed in his father's eyes. "You need to make some decisions, son. Are you going to spend the rest of your life here, waiting for her to wake up? Because I'm sorry, son. I really, really am sorry...but Rosie isn't coming back. She's gone."

Lucas clenched his fists at his sides, and tears burned in his eyes.

Roger stepped forward and put his hands on Lucas's shoulders. Lucas fought the overwhelming urge to push him away. "Or are you ready to answer your pack's call and find where you *really* belong?"

Lucas made the short drive to Hanks Hollow and parked on Lake Street. He clenched his teeth, frustration gnawing at him. Screw his father.

She *would* wake up.

And damn this whole alpha thing. It wasn't his problem. The Beckett pack wasn't his problem.

Was it?

Tears stung his eyes again, and he ground his palms into his sockets as he growled. He wasn't going to figure any of it out tonight. He needed to get it all out of his head. He'd been handed an opportunity to get himself out of the funk he'd been living in, and he was going to take it.

He climbed out of the truck and crossed the sidewalk to the Lake Street back entrance to Miller's. As he ducked through the door, loud music hit his ears. Late at night, the dining room closed, and the bar took center stage. He crossed the darkened dining area, dodging the tables, as he made his way toward the crowded area at the front of the restaurant, where the bar stretched the length of the windowed front wall. He immediately spotted Charlie and gave a short wave.

"Hey, Lucas. Good to see you again, kid." Charlie waved him closer, and Lucas perched on a barstool.

Clearing his throat, Lucas gave a small smile. "I'd like to take you up on that job offer."

A bright smile spread across Charlie's face. "Best news I've heard all day! When can you start?"

"Whenever you need me, I guess."

"Great! I'll put you on the schedule. How does tomorrow night sound? I'll have Becca show you the ropes. In the meantime, want something to eat?"

"Thank you, but I just ate. I'll take a soda, though."

"Coming right up." Charlie tossed a napkin onto the bar and turned toward the tap. He filled a glass with some cola and set it in front of Lucas.

"I'll catch you in a bit, kid." Charlie headed off toward the end of the bar, and Lucas scanned the crowd of locals.

"Lucas?"

He spun to face a tall girl with long, straight brunette hair. She stared at him with eyes lined with dark eyeliner. Something was familiar about her, but Lucas couldn't place how he might know her. In a town this size, he'd probably run into her at least a few times over the years.

"I thought that was you." She flipped her hair behind her shoulder as she slid unsteadily onto the barstool next to him. Her cropped tank top exposed a flat stomach, and a short, tight jean skirt displayed her long, lean legs. She eyed him up again before she smiled coyly. "You don't recognize me, do you?"

Lucas shook his head as he turned back to his soda. The girl reeked of alcohol and was definitely drunk. Charlie didn't serve minors, at least not while he was open. Lucas frowned. Hopefully she didn't have a fake ID. It wasn't like Charlie to fall for something so obvious. "No. Sorry."

"Figures." She rolled her eyes. "You never would give me the time of day." She looked at him a moment longer then huffed out a breath before she tipped forward unsteadily. She caught herself on the bar and giggled. "We were in the same class. We graduated together. Jeez, it was only a few weeks ago."

It dawned on him then. She looked a lot different from how she had in history class. "Cassie?"

She smiled. "I've always wanted to ask you about when you were shot by Mason Lewis's dad." She tipped forward again and put her hand on his arm to steady herself then moved it higher. "Did it leave a scar? Can I see it?"

Heat rushed to his cheeks. He took a sip of his soda as he tried to decide how to respond. "Um. It was a long time ago. The scar is hard to see."

"Well, I'd love to see it sometime." Her hand didn't leave his arm. "I have a confession to make. I always thought you were so hot in high school." She dropped her voice to a whisper as she leaned close to his ear. The stench of cheap beer and heavy perfume assaulted his nose. "You're even hotter now."

Becca breathed a sigh of relief as her shift finally came to an end. It had been a long one, and she was ready to go home and take a bath.

"Hey, Dad." Becca leaned against the bar while her father opened a bottle of beer for one of the regulars. "I think I'm going to head home."

"All right, hon. I'll see you tomorrow. Oh, and hey! You're training someone new."

Becca groaned. "Really? Can't someone else do it?"

"No, I want you to do it. You know him. It's Lucas Beckett."

"Really? He took the job?"

"Yeah. He's down there." Charlie pointed down the bar. "Go say hi. Looks like he could use some rescuing."

Becca glanced in the direction her father had pointed and frowned. Cassie Barnes sat next to Lucas, pawing at his arm. Poor guy looked like he wanted to crawl out of his skin. Cassie used to tease Rosie relentlessly, and Becca couldn't stand her.

Heading in their direction, she called out to Lucas. She nearly laughed at the look of relief on his face.

As she approached, she nudged Cassie away and put a hand on his shoulder. "Dad said you're starting tomorrow. That's so cool!"

Cassie drew in a breath. "Wait, you're going to be working here?" She smiled and winked. "I think I might be coming around a little more often."

"Cassie." Becca sighed as she put a hand on her hip. "You're already here every night. How much more often can you come?"

Cassie ignored Becca, watching Lucas as though she were a hungry dog, and he was a piece of steak. She touched his cheek as she stood. "I'll see you tomorrow."

She swayed her hips in an exaggerated manner as she strolled away. Becca slapped at Lucas's arm when she caught him staring at her butt.

He shook his head. "She have a fake ID or something?"

"Nah." Becca plopped onto the stool Cassie had just vacated. "She's usually drunk by the time she shows up here. Dad's never kicked her out, but I wish he would. Sheriff Hill knows he doesn't serve her, so it hasn't been an issue. Dad says he would rather she come here than go hang out at one of the seedy places outside town, where she might get into trouble." She raised an eyebrow. "She was coming on to you heavy."

"Yeah." Lucas's cheeks reddened again. "That was a little freaky."

"Well, get used to it."

"What do you mean?"

"Lucas, you're young, you're hot, and you're working in a bar." Becca smiled. "Girls are going to be coming on to you a lot."

A worried frown marred his face, and Becca held in a laugh. Most guys would take the job for that fact alone, but Lucas wasn't most guys.

"Don't worry, Lucas. You'll get used to it."

Lucas's frown deepened. "What if I don't want to get used to it?"

"Get used to what?" Sam sat on the other side of Lucas and gave him a shove. "Hey, thanks for offering to let me tag along with you to town. Great show of appreciation for the way I stuck my neck out for you."

Sam's sarcastic tone spoke volumes, and Lucas ducked his head as he shrugged.

Becca straightened. She hadn't even seen Sam come in. "Hey, Sam. I was just telling Lucas he'll need to get used to girls flirting with him."

"Ha! That should be fun to watch." Sam snickered as he turned toward the bar and waved at her father. "Hey, Charlie! I'll take a soda."

"Right! I think working here is about to get really entertaining." Becca giggled.

Lucas groaned. "Did I do something bad to you people? Jeez. I just remembered I need to be somewhere else." He slid off the stool and strolled toward the door, waving goodbye over his shoulder.

"Aw, Lucas, come on!" Becca called after him. "I was just giving you a hard time!"

Laughing, Sam nudged her. "Don't worry about it. He'll be fine. You working?"

"Just got done. What brings you here?" Becca moved to the stool next to Sam.

"I had to get out of that house." Sam cleared his throat as he glanced at Becca. "Do you have to get home right away, or do you want to share a basket of cheese curds?"

Her stomach fluttering with excitement, Becca smiled. "Cheese curds sound good."

~

"You DID NOT!" Becca nearly choked on the fried cheese curd she'd just popped into her mouth. "I thought you were a good brother!"

"I was a jerk!" Sam laughed as he reached for his soda. "I used to tell Rosie that if she found me eight quarters, I would give her a whole dollar. She went hunting through couch cushions and jacket pockets. Lucas had to go and ruin the whole thing by telling her eight quarters was two dollars. He was always running interference."

Something in his eyes shifted as his mind went somewhere far away. If only she could read his thoughts. What would it be like to stroll around in his brain? He was funny, kind, and much smarter than he let on. She swallowed another cheese curd as she glanced at her phone. "Oh my God! It's after midnight. Have we really been talking that long?"

Sam's eyes widened, and he smiled.

God, those eyes.

"It didn't seem like that long. You're really easy to talk to, Becca."

Heat rushed to her cheeks. "I better head home."

"I'll walk you up."

Becca nodded, and they stood then made their way outside.

As Becca paused to unlock the door to her apartment, she could feel his breath against the back of her neck as he leaned in close. She turned toward him. Suddenly, his lips were on hers. A moment of surprise passed quickly before her body relaxed. The kiss was gentle, and she could have sworn she saw fireworks. Pure bliss.

A blush spread across his cheeks after he pulled away. "I've been wanting to do that all night."

Eager to continue where they'd left off, she reached up and touched his neck, pulling him toward her as she leaned in and returned the kiss. Years of longing had led to this moment, and it was just as good as she knew it would be. His lips were so soft.

She reached for the door handle and clumsily opened the door, stumbling backward into the stairwell. He followed her in and closed the door behind them, never breaking contact with her lips as they staggered their way up the staircase. Damn stairs. She kept tripping on them, but Sam's strong arms held her close. He never let her fall.

After fumbling with the knob on the upstairs door for a moment, he opened it, and they moved inside. Excitement and nervousness fluttered in her stomach. Was this really happening? With Sam Hart? Years of wishing...

Her limbs felt like jelly as he pulled her toward the couch and laid her down, moving on top of her. When he broke away for a moment, she searched his eyes. The longing in his gaze churned the desire deep in the pit of her stomach. Her eyes trailed down to his lips as he leaned forward and kissed her again. All her senses came alive. She kissed him back, running her hands through his curls and pulling him toward her.

A groan escaped him, and warmth spread through her at the desire behind the sound he made. Need overpowered everything as she closed her eyes and breathed him in.

Sunlight warmed Sam's face, and he stretched his arms above his head as he cracked his eyes open. A fluffy white comforter lay before him, and through a window that wasn't his, a beautiful view of Mingan Lake greeted him.

Oh shit.

Slowly, he moved his head to the side. Long blond tresses sprawled out over the pillow next to him. The tranquil look on Becca's face drew him in, and he fought the urge to kiss her bare shoulders. God, she was beautiful.

Last night was incredible.

But this was wrong. If Amos found out...

Throwing back the covers, Sam silently slid out of bed. Hunting through the sea of clothes that littered the floor, he found his pants. He tiptoed around the room, looking for the rest of his clothes. He spotted one sock then the other. His shirt. God, where was his shirt? After a bit more searching, he located his boxers.

After stepping lightly out to the living room, he found his shirt next to the sofa. Dressing as he moved toward the door, he threw on his shoes and opened the door as quietly as he could. Then he silently closed it behind him and crept down the stairs and out the front door.

Blinking into the sunlight, he jogged down the boardwalk and turned the corner into the alley next to Miller's. He ran through it to the street and jumped into his SUV, started it up, and pulled onto the road.

What the hell was wrong with him? He shouldn't have let anything happen with Becca. But God, last night...

He shook his head as he thought about Amos's threat. The image of his alpha's sharp wolf teeth tearing into Becca's neck caused a spike of fear, and his breathing quickened. No. He couldn't let that happen.

As he neared the entrance to Hart House, he hit the button on the opener for the gate and steered the SUV up the long, tree-lined driveway. As Hart House came into view, his stomach tightened. The pack would be eating breakfast. Amos would know he'd been out all night.

Damn.

He parked the SUV and took his time walking across the driveway and up the walkway to the front steps. He jogged up the stairs and crossed the large veranda to the front door. Taking a deep breath, he silently opened the door and peeked inside. It was impossible to sneak up on a house full of werewolves with enhanced hearing. Not sure why he was trying so hard to be quiet.

He cleared his throat as he wandered down the hallway to the dining room. Lucas raised an eyebrow at him, and Michael smirked, but everyone stayed quiet as he sat at the table. Scooping some eggs onto his plate, he waited.

He didn't have to wait long.

"Where the hell were you?" Amos didn't look at him as he asked the question. Sam opened his mouth to reply, but Amos cut him off. "Don't lie to me. You reek of sex."

His cheeks heated. "I was with someone, yes. I was careful."

A long, deep breath escaped Amos. "Did I not make myself clear the other day?"

"You did. I was careful. There won't be any offspring."

"I'm not stupid. I know you boys sleep around. How many times did I watch your dad let you go off and date some little slut when you were in high school?" Amos turned his glare to Michael. "And I know you've had enough drunk sex to put a porn star to shame." He shook his head. "I can't watch you boys every second of every day. But if I catch you, or if you bring home some knocked-up whore, there will be hell to pay."

~

Closing his eyes, Sam ignored the buzzing of his phone, then he opened them again and tried to focus on the movie in front of him. His stomach clenched. He was such an ass.

"You're buzzing again." Next to him, Daniel grabbed a handful of popcorn from the bowl on the coffee table. "Who are we avoiding?"

"No one."

"Right. Are you sure it isn't the same person who kept you out all night?" Daniel spoke around a mouthful of popcorn.

"Mind your own business."

Daniel swallowed. "Yikes. Sore subject. Sorry."

Guilt washed over him. Daniel was the nicest guy on the planet. He didn't deserve to have Sam's frustration taken out on him. "I'm sorry, Daniel. I just don't want to talk about it, okay?"

"Okay."

On the TV screen, Tom Hanks was crying over a volleyball. Sam groaned. "Who chose this movie?"

"You did."

Oh yeah. Dammit. Should have gone with Daniel's suggestion of something funny. He wasn't in the mood for this.

The sofa dipped next to him, and he turned as Lucas leaned back into the cushions and pinned him with a dirty stare. Sam sighed. "What's with you?"

"You know my first night of work is going to be awkward as hell, right?" Lucas crossed his arms. "Are you seriously avoiding her now? She's going to be pissed, and she's going to take it out on me."

"She's not going to take it out on you. Get over yourself." Sam turned the TV up.

"Grow up, Sam!" Lucas yelled. "This isn't one of your high school conquests. It's Becca."

"Wait, Becca? As in Rosie's best friend?" Daniel raised his voice. "Sam..."

Growling, Sam looked toward the hallway. "Would you guys shut up! I don't want Amos to know."

"Grow a pair. And stop being an ass." Lucas stood and stomped out of the room.

Growling again, Sam jumped up from the couch and threw the remote onto the cushions. "I'm going out."

After he stomped out to the SUV and tore out of the garage and down the driveway, he turned toward

Hanks Hollow. His intended destination was Becca's place, but the closer he got to town, the more he lost his nerve. What on earth could he say to her? Nothing would sound right. Nothing would make what he'd done right. He'd pulled the ultimate asshole move.

Making a last-minute decision, he steered the SUV onto the highway leading out of town, toward the hospital.

SEVENTEEN
BECCA

"Are you kidding me?" Becca slammed her silverware drawer shut and stared up at the ceiling. She'd bought a frozen pizza the other night, only to realize when she got home that she didn't have a pizza pan. She went out and bought a pizza pan yesterday morning and successfully baked her first frozen pizza today for lunch—only to now realize she didn't have a pizza cutter.

Charlie had given her an advance on her next few paychecks a few days ago and told her to go shopping for what she needed for her new place. She'd never realized how many things she would need to live on her own. Every time she thought she had it all under control, something came up, and she realized she needed to go back to the store.

Growling in frustration, she opened the silverware drawer again just so that she could slam it shut even harder.

But the missing pizza cutter wasn't the real reason for her frustration.

Dammit, Sam Hart. Asshole. Never in a million years had she thought he would be the guy who would sleep with her then never call again. Sneaking out before she woke up was just the tip of the iceberg. She'd been so hurt and embarrassed to wake up to an empty bed. Then the creep wouldn't return her texts when she asked him what was wrong.

God, she'd spent years in love with Sam. Then last night...

This hurt. This hurt so much.

She'd spent most of her morning crying into her pillow. Cold loneliness came over her, and she wanted—needed—someone to talk to. She had plenty of friends she could call to come over and keep her company, but she craved the presence of her best friend. Her closest confidant.

The one lying in a coma in the hospital.

"Screw it." Becca tore a chunk of pizza off like a cavewoman. Greasy cheese and toppings dripped over her hand as she shoved the piece into her mouth. Standing in the kitchen, eating pizza like a messy toddler, she came to a decision.

She needed to see Rosie. And she needed to see her today.

After wiping grease and pizza sauce from her hands, she headed to her room and threw on a pair of jeans and a short-sleeved top. Then she moved to the bathroom and applied some makeup and straightened her hair before she put on her shoes and hurried out the door.

"Ugh. I knew I should have brought some nail polish with me." Becca fought tears as she examined Rosie's delicate fingers. "Every time I painted your nails, you had them dirt covered and chipped by the next day. Maybe now, you could keep a mani looking beautiful for more than a day." She brushed her fingers over Rosie's. "I'll bring some next time. And I promise next time won't be long from now." Becca ran her hands over her face and sighed. "I have so much to tell you. It's been a rollercoaster of a week, I tell ya.

"First of all, I have a confession to make. I have a thing for your brother. I mean a big thing. Like... colossal. But don't worry. I thought the feeling was mutual for a minute there, but it turns out I was wrong. Big surprise, right? Like Sam Hart would date his little sister's annoying friend.

"I got my own apartment. Dad gave me the space above the restaurant. It's so cool, Rosie. I wish you could see it." Becca took a deep breath. "But it's missing something. You. You would make the best roommate. You know that? It's so quiet and lonely. I need late-night gossip and movie marathons and pop-corn fights. Like our old sleepovers. Remember? We stayed up all night, then Dad would drop us off on Main Street on his way to the restaurant. We had breakfast at the diner, then we went to every snack shop downtown and filled ourselves up until we were sick."

A tear dripped down Becca's cheek, and she wiped it away. "Enough with the stroll down memory lane. I'm here to read to you. I brought a boring old wildlife magazine. You see how much I love you? I'm going to read this boring old drivel because I know it's what you like to read. Ugh. You're so weird. I can't even with you, Rosie."

Becca shook her head as she pulled the magazine out of her purse, then she leaned back in the chair and started to read.

Sam's legs were numb. Really numb. His butt was numb too. He'd been sitting on the bathroom floor inside Rosie's hospital room for more than an hour.

He'd come in to relieve himself just as Becca had stopped by to visit Rosie. He hadn't meant to eavesdrop, but he paused with his hand on the door while she talked to his sister. Heat rushed to his cheeks when she confessed her "thing" for him.

Memories rushed back to him when she talked about their sleepovers. Rosie always came back home as sick as a dog. It was kind of funny to hear Becca's account of how that happened.

Pretty soon, it was too late for him to open the door. She would know he'd been listening in. He would just have to wait for her to leave.

Then she'd brought out the damn magazine. How could Rosie read that crap? That was when he sat on the floor and tried to make himself comfortable. Damn cramped little bathroom was too small for him to stretch his legs out.

He sat and listened for another ten minutes as she read about possums and venom or something like that.

He leaned his head back and let himself get lost in the sound of her voice. How much longer was she going to read?

Silence on the other side of the door caught his attention. Was she leaving? Footsteps. Sam's heart rate sped up as he realized the footsteps were headed his way. Was she coming to use the bathroom?

Shit!

He reached up to lock the door, but he was too late. The door swung open, and he looked up at Becca's surprised squeal.

"Sam? What the hell are you doing?" Becca took a step back, her mouth opening and closing like she was searching for words. "Have you been here this whole time? What the hell is wrong with you? Were you listening? The *whole* time?"

Sam fumbled his way to his feet and stumbled on his numb legs. "Becca, I'm sorry. It was an accident!"

"An accident? How do you accidentally hide in the bathroom?"

"I heard you come in, and I was going to come out, but then you started talking—"

"Get out!"

"Becca, wait—"

"No, I mean..." Becca huffed and crossed her arms. "Get out of the bathroom. I really have to pee."

Sam blinked. "Right. Okay."

He stepped out, and Becca moved inside, closing the door behind her.

"I'll just be out here, okay?"

"Fine!" Becca's voice was muffled by the door.

After a flush and the sound of running water, Becca whipped the door open. "I can't believe you, Sam."

"Look, can we just... talk?"

"Now you want to talk?"

Sam flinched. "I meant to text you back. I just—"

"Don't give me that. You had no intention of texting me back. If you didn't want to see me again, that's fine, but have enough respect to tell me instead of just ghosting me like a pansy-ass loser."

"That's fair. Look, can we just talk..." Sam glanced behind him to Rosie's bed. "In the cafeteria? I don't want to argue in front of her. Please."

Becca's gaze drifted over to Rosie, and her shoulders sagged as she frowned. "Yeah. Okay."

SAM STABBED at a piece of fruit and sighed. "I really am sorry."

Becca looked around. Everywhere but Sam's face. "Yeah. You said that."

The outdoor seating area was situated next to a large patch of flowering bushes. A walkway bordered by small benches split the garden.

"It really was an accident."

"You said that too."

"And about your texts—"

"You don't have to explain, Sam." Becca crossed her arms. "I got the hint."

"That's just it, though." Sam sighed. "I didn't mean to ghost you. I just... It's complicated."

Becca raised an eyebrow, and Sam fought the urge to smack his head. The words sounded hollow and stupid in his own ears. Why was this so hard? He wasn't used to getting tongue-tied around girls. "I really like you, Becca."

"Could have fooled me." Tears filled Becca's eyes.

"I should have texted you back. Or called you. Or

stopped by. I got scared, okay?" He flinched as the truth came out. Maybe Amos wasn't the only reason he'd run away. She was special. Someone who had the ability to hurt him. And damn if that didn't scare the ever-living shit out of him.

"Scared of what?" Becca's brow creased, not from anger but from curiosity.

"I've never been in a relationship with someone I really cared about, okay?"

At Becca's skeptical raise of an eyebrow, Sam sighed. His high school reputation was coming back to bite him in the ass.

"I know I dated a lot in high school, but that was different. It was just fun and games. Never anything serious. This..." Sam pointed back and forth between himself and Becca. "This isn't fun and games. This isn't superficial. This seems like it could be... real."

And he had to hide her from his murderous alpha. But that wasn't a part he could share. Thinking about Amos, Sam hesitated. What was he doing? Why was he pursuing this? His gaze flicked over to the garden again. Rosie would love to wander down that walkway and admire the flowers.

Rosie. What would she say if he told her he blew Becca off? She'd tear him a new one. His gaze flicked back to Becca. Her beautiful blue eyes searched his face, and her supple pink lips parted slightly, like she was about to speak. They looked so soft.

Sam leaned forward. Becca didn't move, but he could sense her holding her breath. Hope blossomed in his chest. His lips brushed over hers. They were so soft. She responded, and their lips melded together. He leaned in and put his hands on her cheeks, pulling her toward him. A strong urge pulsed inside him, and he pressed himself into her.

With a sharp gasp, she pulled away. "I'm still mad at you, Sam Hart."

"I know."

"Furious."

"I know."

"You really hurt me."

That one pierced his heart. He hadn't meant to hurt her. "I'm so sorry, Becca. Will you give me another chance? Please?"

Forgiveness shouldn't have come so easily. What did that say about her? Was she that much of a pushover? After they'd left the hospital, she agreed to let him wait for her in her apartment while she worked her shift and started Lucas's training.

When she'd come upstairs at the end of the night, he had a candlelit dinner waiting for her, like something from a movie. As she stood in the doorway, speechless, he'd pulled her in for a long kiss, and just like that, her anger melted away.

Now, as Becca watched Sam sleep next to her, she knew she had no choice but to forgive him. What could she say? It was *Sam*. She was falling in love with him. She'd always had a mad crush on him, but now...

Please, God, don't let her get hurt. If any man in the world had the power to destroy her, it was the one sleeping next to her.

She sighed as she turned her gaze out the window. The lights from the boardwalk barely pierced the dark abyss over the lake. She had such a great view out her window each morning, but at night, the eeriness of that dark stretch of nothingness that hung over the empty water and the sparsely populated forest beyond sent a chill down her spine.

"What are you thinking about?"

"Jesus, Sam!" Becca put a hand to her thundering heart. "You scared me to death."

Sam chuckled as he pushed Becca's hair off her shoulders. "Sorry. I didn't mean to scare you." He sat up slowly and ran his hand down her bare arm. When he leaned forward to kiss her shoulder, he chuckled again as goose bumps rose on her skin, and he peppered her shoulder with more kisses.

"Mmm." Becca closed her eyes and tipped her head back as his kisses reached her neck. "That feels so good."

"So, I'm forgiven?"

"You're on probation." Becca cracked her eyes open. "Don't pull that again."

"Never."

He pulled her toward him and wrapped his arms around her as he kissed the other side of her neck. She tilted her head, inviting him to continue.

His touch was whisper soft as he ran his fingers up and down her arms. "I don't want to screw this up."

She tipped her head up to look into his eyes and held his gaze. "Then don't."

The night of ecstasy that followed brought her to a place she never dreamed she'd go. The first time with him had been amazing, but the second time was extraordinary. She couldn't imagine that heaven held a candle to it.

When she woke the next morning, she held her breath as she glanced at the empty spot next to her. Fear tightened her chest before she heard the clang of dishes. Smiling, she sat up and reached for her white silk robe then slipped it on as she padded out to the kitchen. Her head was somewhere up in the clouds, still floating on the pleasure of the night before.

"Hey, you." Sam reached for her hand and pulled her into a one-armed hug. "I was going to make you breakfast, but you don't have anything."

"Yeah. I'm slowly trying to accumulate things, but it's a work in progress."

"Diner or your dad's?"

"Definitely diner. I'm not ready for my dad to see me bring you to breakfast just yet." Plus, the diner had better breakfast, though she would never say that out loud. Her dad's restaurant was the place to go for lunch and dinner, but the omelets and pancakes left something to be desired.

After a quick shower, Becca dressed in a tank top and a pair of shorts while Sam lounged in the living room, watching television. After dabbing some makeup on her face, she started the long process of drying her long, thick hair. Ten minutes later, as she strolled out to the living room, Sam stood from the couch to greet her. He ran a hand through her freshly dried hair, and she smiled at the way his fingers played with the strands.

"Ready?"

Sam held out his hand, and Becca laced her fingers through his. Their hands remained locked together as they left the apartment and headed toward Main Street. The shops were just starting to open, and Becca could feel the stares as they strolled down the sidewalk hand in hand. People talked in small towns. As Charlie Miller's daughter, Becca was well known. And everyone knew Sam. Becca could hear the gossip starting already. Rumors of their impending marriage would probably beat them to the diner.

Heat flooded Becca's cheeks, and she bit her lip to hide a smile.

"You okay?"

Sam gave her a funny look, and Becca's cheeks heated even more. Something was different about the way he looked at her. He'd never looked at her like that before. She liked it.

A warm feeling filled her stomach as her chest swelled. Her hand tightened around his. "I'm great."

TWENTY

LUCAS

"So... what? You can't drink it, but you can serve it? Don't seem right to me."

Ernie drained his bottle of pilsner and slid the empty bottle toward Lucas, who caught it before it tipped off the end of the bar. He tossed the bottle into the trash can and reached into the cooler for another then set it down in front of Ernie as the man smirked at him.

"You even have pubic hair yet, kid?"

Heat crept into Lucas's cheeks, and Ernie laughed.

"What difference does it make, Ernie?" Charlie called out from the other side of the bar, where he was shuffling through piles of paperwork. "You're getting your beer. Do you really care who hands it to you?"

The midafternoon crowd was thin, the regulars just starting to trickle in after finishing work for the day. Most of them came from the distribution warehouse outside town.

"Bartenders are supposed to be world-weary old men you can tell all your problems to." Ernie eyed Lucas. "What does this kid know about real-world problems?"

"Ernie." Charlie stopped what he was doing and stared at the old man over his reading glasses. "Not once in the twenty years you've been warming that seat have you told me anything about your problems. Shut up already. The kid is doing me a favor. Don't scare him off."

"Whatever. Just keep 'em coming till I say stop, and don't try to sell me on any of that new-age craft shit you've been pushing on the vacationers." Ernie took another swig and nodded a greeting to some of his fellow barflies as they bellied up to their usual seats.

"I wouldn't do that, Ernie." Lucas grinned. "This stuff is too rich for your blood."

Ernie cursed over the sound of Charlie's laugh. "You're too new to be dishing out the sass, kid. Keep your trap shut."

Lucas raised his hands in surrender. "You got it."

After Lucas had worked almost every afternoon for two weeks, the regulars were finally starting to warm up to him. The ribbing Ernie had given him was much better than the silent glares he'd been receiving.

Spikes of bright sun split across the dark floor as more regulars filtered through the door. Lucas looked out the window that stretched the length of the wall behind him. The lake water sparkled under the sun, and he briefly wished he could be outside, enjoying the weather. He rolled his eyes as he caught sight of Sam and Becca making out on the pier.

Get a room.

The two of them had become an item, and everyone was talking about it. A lot of the guys gave Charlie a hard time about Sam stealing his daughter's virtue, but the easy smile on Charlie's face spoke volumes. He was pleased with the pairing.

"Watch it, kid." Ernie's low, gravelly voice held a hint of amusement. "Your stalker is coming."

Lucas cursed under his breath as Cassie Barnes strolled in, her dark hair blowing around her shoulders as a breeze blew in behind her. Her dark eyes darted straight toward Lucas, and a wide, cat-like grin stretched across her face as she strolled toward the bar and slid onto an empty barstool. "Hi, Lucas."

"Hi, Cassie." Lucas forced a smile. "Diet cola?"

"Actually..." Cassie leaned forward and propped her chin on her hand. "I think I might try one of those nonalcoholic beers you've been talking about. Since Charlie won't serve me the real stuff." Cassie raised her voice and glanced at Charlie.

"You're eighteen, Cassie. I have a liquor license to protect." Charlie gave her a tight smile. "When you hit twenty-one, I'll have to double my supply."

"Ha-ha." Cassie reached a long arm across the bar and gave Charlie a playful shove before she turned back to Lucas. "So how about it, Lucas? What do you recommend?"

As annoyed as Lucas was by her presence, he couldn't contain the excitement of turning someone on to one of the new brews he'd gotten Charlie to order. "My favorite is the Little Lumberjack Stout, but I know you like pilsner, so you might want something a little lighter. There's a nonalcoholic lager you should try."

Lucas fished the beer from the cooler and plopped it in front of Cassie.

She smiled and took a tentative sip. "Wow, that's really good! You can't even tell there's no alcohol in it."

"How would you know what alcohol tastes like, Cassie? You're too young to drink, if I recall." Sheriff Craig Hill sat on the empty stool next to Cassie and nodded at Lucas.

"I've *heard* a lot about what it tastes like." Cassie gave another cat-like grin, and Craig rolled his eyes.

"The usual, Craig?" Lucas didn't wait for an answer as he reached behind him for the half-full bottle of Jack. He grabbed a glass from under the counter as Craig nodded then set the glass on the bar in front of the sheriff and filled it half full with the amber-colored whiskey. "Anything exciting happen today?"

Craig rolled his shoulders. "Nah. Nothing. Heard from one of my pals over in Forest County, though. They've had more livestock turn up dead. Looks like a wolf again."

"Wolf? That so?" Burt Toller, another regular, glanced at the sheriff. "Wolf attacks have been all over the news. Strange how they've been going after the livestock. Never seen nothing like it. Glad it's staying away from here."

"Darnedest thing, though." The sheriff scratched his head. "It's happening straight east and straight west but nothing around here."

Unease cramped Lucas's stomach. Sam needed to know about this. Glancing out the window, he groaned. Still making out with Becca on the pier. They had to come up for air sometime.

"Hey, Charlie. You mind if I take fifteen?"

"Go ahead, Lucas, but don't be long. We're about to get busy."

Lucas gave a short nod. As he headed toward the door, a hand shot out and caught his arm.

"Can I talk to you, Lucas?" Cassie blinked up at him and bit her lip. "Please?"

Glancing out the window, Lucas sighed. It wouldn't hurt to tell Sam a little later. "I guess so."

His stomach flipped as Cassie ran her hand down his arm. Her hands were soft, her touch gentle. Goose bumps rose on his skin as she laced her fingers through his. She held his gaze, her dark eyes staring into his as she pulled him toward the vacant tables at the back of the restaurant. She made her way to the booths that lined the wall and slid into one, pulling him down to sit next to her. Her gaze returned to his face, her eyes taking on a lusty quality that made Lucas nervous.

Clearing his throat, Lucas looked back toward the bar area. No one was watching, and he was glad. "What did you want to talk about, Cassie?"

"Don't do that."

"Huh?" Lucas looked at her in confusion.

"Don't pretend you don't know why I brought you back here, Lucas." Her fingers touched his chin, pulling him down toward her. Her other hand reached behind him, and her fingers ran through his hair, massaging his head. He closed his eyes as his scalp tingled under her touch. When her lips met his, he didn't fight it or pull away. He accepted it, parting his lips and letting her in. Reaching a hand forward, he touched her waist, his fingers brushing against the skin on her back. His body reacted, and he pulled her closer.

He hadn't felt urges like this since...

As he pulled away, his heart thundered loudly in his ears. What was he doing? Something inside him screamed. The mate bond within him roared to life. No longer a flickering flame that warmed him and brought light to the darkest corners of his mind, the fire raged in fury at his betrayal. He stumbled out of the booth and braced himself against the wall. Breathing became difficult as tears stung his eyes.

"Lucas? What's wrong?"

Cassie's voice sounded far away as he stumbled toward the bathroom. How could he do this? His stomach twisted. He had to get to the toilet. The burger he'd had for lunch was on its way up. He swallowed and increased his pace, bulldozing through the bathroom door and into the stall, where he heaved out the contents of his stomach.

All he could see was Rosie's sweet smile. Her curly red hair. He was an asshole. How could he do this to her? Guilt gnawed at him. Always guilt. It ate at him every moment of every day, like flesh-eating bugs. Nothing would ever be the same, and it was his fault.

His fault.

Something broke. Something he'd been holding on to for so long.

Hope.

The hope that this was just temporary. Just a nightmare. That Rosie was coming back to him, and it would all be the same. It wouldn't be. He wasn't the same.

The person he used to be died the day she fell off the cliff.

Rosie squinted in frustration at the thick, never-ending crop of trees that stood before her. Rubbing her tired, dirty feet, she studied the shallow cuts that formed small fissures along her soles, the result of sharp twigs and pine needles that she'd been picking out of her skin all day. The lacy fringe of her dress fell over her foot as she examined it, and she flung it out of the way with a huff.

Stupid dress.

Stupid woods.

Stupid dreams.

How long had she been walking in what she hoped was the direction of the house, only to find herself back at the oak tree again? She gazed up at the snippets of blue sky she could see through the tops of the trees. There had been no sunset or sunrise, but it felt like she'd been here forever.

Dreams came and went. It was starting to get hard to tell what was real. Was any of it real?

If this was all a dream, she was taking a really long time to wake up. If it was real, how on earth had she ended up in the middle of the woods, wearing a dress she knew for a fact she didn't own, talking to her father, who came and went like the Cheshire Cat?

Her father...who was dead.

Her nose stung, and the forest blurred as the truth of it smacked into her yet again. She'd seen him lying there, his lifeless eyes staring into the sky. She squeezed her eyes shut and felt tears drip down her cheeks.

Daddy.

This couldn't be real. This was some messed-up, drug-induced haze. She'd learned about the dangers of hallucinogens in health class and vowed never to touch them with a ten-foot pole. No drugs had touched her lips. At least, not that she was aware of. But how else could she explain having a conversation with a hippie woman and a half man, half deer? Their words echoed in her ears.

Curling up at the base of her oak again, she hugged her knees to her chest. Another tear dripped down her cheek. Her chin wobbled, and she held in a sob. How was she supposed to bring werewolves and witches together? She couldn't even find her way out of the forest she'd lived in her entire life.

Her thoughts strayed to Stuart and what she'd seen him do. She squeezed her eyes shut and tried to erase the memory from her mind. Tried to cling to the good memories she had with him when she'd listened to his stories and fallen asleep in his lap.

That was her Stuart. Not the one she'd seen in the basement. Her Stuart wouldn't do those horrible things.

A line of ants drew her attention as they crawled over dead pine needles and leaves toward her feet. Soon, they would be crawling up her toes, but she couldn't get herself to move. Instead, she wearily stared at them and silently wished for them to change course.

To her immense surprise, they did.

The head ant veered off, and his little troops followed. Strange. She furrowed her brow as she watched. Driven by a surge of fascination, she sat up. In her mind, she plotted a course for the little ant parade, over the oak's roots and up the side of the trunk. She watched in fascination as the ants did exactly as she silently instructed.

"That's right, Rosie. They're listening to you."

Her heart leaping to her throat, Rosie screeched as she backed farther into the tree's roots and stared up at the woman who stood before her. Long red hair spilled over the woman's shoulders. Her flawless ivory skin made her look like a Greek statue, and her heart-shaped pink lips curved into a bright smile. Rosie knew that smile. She knew that face. She'd seen it in a dozen photos that lined her grandma's shelves.

"Mom?"

Mom. The word was foreign on her tongue, but what else could she call the woman who stood in front of her? Gwen? That didn't seem right either.

At the woman's nod, a hiccupped sob escaped Rosie. "How are you here? I don't understand."

"Rosie, it's really you." Joy radiated through the tears glistening in her mother's eyes as she knelt in front of Rosie and reached a delicate hand out to grasp Rosie's dirty fingers.

A wave of euphoria rushed through her body at her mother's touch. She closed her eyes and took it in.

"I have so much I want to tell you." Gwen's voice rose with excitement. "I can't believe I'm really sitting here with you. This is—"

"You're dead." The words sounded cold and horrible, and Rosie flinched when she said them. Her gaze trailed around to the forest. The thick, never-ending forest that had her trapped. A thought occurred to her. "Am I dead? Is this heaven?"

Another smile stretched across Gwen's beautiful face. So beautiful…just like Rosie's father had said she was. "No, Rosie. This isn't heaven, but it's not your world. You just need to stay here for a while. Until it's safe."

"Until it's safe? That's what everyone keeps saying. Why isn't it safe at home?" Dread filled her gut. "What about Lucas? Is he safe? What about the rest of the pack?"

"They'll be okay." Gwen sat back and folded her hands in her lap. She closed her eyes and tilted her head up to let the sun warm her face. "Sam will take care of them."

"Sam? Sam can't... not on his own." Rosie shook her head. "He needs me. I have to go back."

Her mother gently raised her hands as though trying to calm a scared animal then reached a hand forward. The moment her fingers swept over Rosie's arm, Rosie's anxiety melted away. "It's not time yet. Besides, we have a lot of work to do."

Rosie eyed her mother warily. "What kind of work?"

"Your magic. We have a lot to cover."

"My magic? What about my magic? Grandma has taught me—"

"Grandma has just scratched the surface, Rosie." Gwen gestured to the line of ants. "She has no idea what you're capable of. You have so much potential in you, but there's so much more you have to learn."

Her mother's eyes were a deep emerald green, like her grandma's. Rosie studied them as her mother spoke. Her entire life, she'd wondered what her mother was like. Now, here she was, right in front of her—talking to her.

Tentatively, she reached a hand out to touch her mother's cheek. "Grandma has told me so much about you, but there's so much more I would love to know."

"You have no idea how much I wish I could have

been there for you." The green glistened as tears sprang to her eyes again. "You're perfect. You know that? You're so much more than I could ever have dreamed. To touch you, to be here with you...maybe this *is* heaven." She smiled again. "There will be time for us. But we have work to do too."

"Work? What work? Bringing the witches and the werewolves together?" Rosie shook her head and swiped away the tears that spilled down her cheeks. "They have the wrong girl. I can't do that."

"You're *already* doing it. You just don't know you are."

Rosie closed her eyes as her mother ran a hand through her hair. The soothing touch was like nothing she'd ever felt. Was this what it was like to have a mother? Did a mother's touch always feel so good? Was this what she'd been missing all these years? Her chest ached, and her breath caught on a sob. Her mother's hand drifted down to her cheek, and Rosie leaned into it.

"You're really here?"

Gwen nodded. "The gods sent me to help prepare you."

"I don't know what's real anymore." Rosie let another sob escape. "I'm scared."

"This is all in your head, but it's also real." Gwen giggled and rolled her eyes. "I know that doesn't make a lot of sense, but trust me. The gods are sending you messages. They want you to listen."

"I was never really sure they existed." Rosie wiped tears and snot from her face.

"They exist. The God of Hunting and the Mother Goddess created the Chosen to help humans when they were most vulnerable. Back when people lived close with the earth, and everything was in balance. The werewolves helped the human men to hunt. The witches helped the human women to care for their tribes."

"I guess there weren't any women hunters back then?" Rosie wrinkled her nose.

Gwen rolled her eyes and laughed. "No. Hunting was only for men."

"How progressive."

"Hey, we're talking ancient times here, Rosie."

"Were there any Chosen who were half witch and half werewolf? Like me?"

Gwen shook her head. "No. The werewolves and the witches mated with one another to produce more Chosen. The newborn males were always werewolves, and the newborn females were always witches."

"Then why..." Rosie furrowed her brow. "Why am I so different?"

"Do you think you would have drawn the attention of the werewolf world if you weren't a female werewolf? The gods had a plan for you right from the beginning,."

Air left her lungs in a huff. She was a prop. A pawn to be used in a higher plan. Should she be offended or feel blessed? The entire thing sounded so bizarre, yet it also sort of made sense. Ever since she'd woken up in the forest in the strange white dress, nothing had been right, but slowly, pieces were falling into place. Pieces that had been missing from her life for the past sixteen years.

"I have so much I want to ask you." Rosie whispered the words and looked into her mother's face, afraid she would disappear.

Gwen watched her for a moment then settled in next to her, making herself comfortable. "Like what?"

Rosie took a deep, steadying breath. "Did you know Dad was a werewolf?"

"Not at first." Gwen chewed on her lip and furrowed her brow. Her eyes drifted off toward the trees as though lost in thought. "But I knew he was special."

"How did you find out what he was?"

"The gods came to me in a dream. They told me you were coming."

Rosie gaped at her mother. "Seriously?"

"Seriously."

"You know this all sounds ridiculous, right? Like a vivid dream that's just way too out there to be real?"

Gwen pressed her lips together as though suppressing a laugh. "I do know that. At first, I thought the same thing. But then I sensed your father's energy. It was familiar in a way it hadn't been before. It had always been...different. But after the dream, it was familiar. His energy felt similar to the energy I felt from the God."

"You mean the half man, half deer?" Rosie raised an eyebrow. "That didn't freak you out?"

"Oh, it definitely freaked me out." Gwen laughed again. "Almost as much as what they told me. That you were coming. That I wouldn't survive."

"Wait." Rosie sat up straight. "You knew you would die giving birth to me?"

Gwen nodded as she pushed a strand of Rosie's hair out of her face.

"And you went through with it anyway?" Rosie's heart raced. "You could have terminated the pregnancy and lived."

Gwen's brow furrowed. "After the visit from the gods, I could feel you inside me. Your energy. Suddenly, I was filled with so much more love than I've ever felt before. I knew you were something special. Giving birth to you was the most important thing in the world to me. I was devastated I wouldn't get to see you grow up. But I would do it again a thousand times."

"And you didn't tell Dad?"

She shook her head. "He wouldn't have understood."

"He missed you all the time." Rosie lowered her eyes. "He really loved you."

"I love him too."

The waver of her mother's voice made Rosie look at her again. Gwen's eyes glimmered with fresh tears.

"I miss him. I see him in you. In your eyes, of course. But also in your personality. You got the best of him. You got the best of both of us."

"Your magic and Dad's wolf." Something fluttered in Rosie's stomach when she said the words. She had been chosen for something. Whether or not she felt worthy or ready didn't matter. A sense of responsibility tightened her muscles. "They're special gifts. I'm blessed to have them. I need to use them for good."

Her mother's smile radiated pride Rosie had never realized she craved.

"What do I need to do?"

THERE WAS SOMETHING ABOUT TYING HIS sneakers in the morning that made Lucas's feet twitch in anticipation for his run. His legs tingled, and a current of energy zapped through his body. He hopped on the balls of his feet before he jogged toward the stairs and descended, taking them two at a time. Flipping the hood up on his sweatshirt, he reached for the front door and jerked his hand back in surprise when the handle jiggled, and the door opened a crack. Sam peeked his head inside, and Lucas bit back a grin.

"Third time this week, Sam. You know that Amos knows you're staying out all night, right?"

"I know. But I need to keep up some pretense of being sneaky about it." Sam moved into the house and shut the door behind him. "Has he said anything?"

Lucas shrugged. "Not really. He just walks around looking pissed when you're not here."

As the summer months passed by, Sam had been spending less and less time at Hart House. No one talked about where he was, but they all knew. He'd practically moved into Becca Miller's apartment. The two of them were joined at the hip, and Lucas had a front-row view of their unapologetic PDA every evening he had a shift at Miller's.

"I'm surprised he hasn't called me out on it yet." Sam stuffed his hands into his pockets. Traces of worry wrinkled his forehead. "I haven't exactly been keeping it a secret."

"Are you kidding? Amos is afraid of you, Sam." When Sam scoffed, Lucas shook his head. "Come on. He knows we all follow you. He needs to watch his step. If he pisses you off, he risks pissing off the rest of the pack. He's just our pretend alpha, and he knows it."

Sam leaned against the wall and glared at Lucas. "What the hell are you talking about?"

"You're so dense sometimes." Lucas shook his head again. "Sam, you might not be alpha in title, but you know everyone answers to you. Do you really think anyone would go to Amos about anything? No. They go to you."

"I'm not alpha," Sam said through clenched teeth.

Lucas sighed. Why was Sam fighting this so hard? As soon as the thought crossed his mind, Lucas internally flinched. Was he being hypocritical? Nah. Lucas's reluctance to take his place as alpha was different. Much different.

"Keep telling yourself that, Sam. As soon as you come to your senses, the rest of us will be ready."

Lucas reached for the front door and gave Sam a weak smile before he pulled it open. He squinted into the early-morning sun as he stepped onto the veranda. Bouncing on his feet again, he jogged down the stairs and started down the driveway at a steady pace.

Breathing in through his nose and out through his mouth, Lucas increased his pace as he turned onto the road. The pavement lay before him, framed by evergreens. He took another deep breath in through his nose, and the smell that hit him made him freeze in his tracks. Glancing around, he sniffed the air again.

Werewolves. The smell was unmistakable. Not the Hart pack. He gave another sniff. He'd smelled that stench before.

Cramers.

The realization hit him just as a mass of fur and muscle knocked him off his feet. His head smacked into the ground, his cheek scraping painfully against the rough pavement. It only took a moment for his dazed thoughts to come back to him as a low growl rumbled inches away, and hot breath hit his face. He opened his eyes and stared into the nostrils of an enormous wolf. Scrambling backward, he thought of shifting, but before he could move, sharp teeth sank into his leg, tearing at his flesh. He screamed at the white-hot agony that ripped through him.

"Don't shift, or George will tear out your throat." Bruce Cramer stood at the edge of the road, his cold eyes glaring.

Lucas's gaze flitted back over to the wolf. Blood caked the fur around his mouth. Much more blood than what poured from Lucas's leg. The fresh metallic smell hit him. They'd killed recently. He glanced back at Bruce. "What did you do?"

"Just a little payback." Bruce took a step onto the road. "The rogue belongs to the Harts. There's no mistaking it."

"None of us have left our territory."

"I know *you* haven't." Bruce rolled his eyes. "You still reek of the Becketts, even after all this time. So does your father. The rogue smells like a Hart."

"No one has left."

"Bullshit! Someone is coming onto our land and

killing livestock. It's got the hunters in an uproar, and they're stalking our territory every day. We can't go out running without coming across imbeciles with guns."

Lucas narrowed his gaze, but he stayed silent.

"Conveniently, the only area spared of the attacks is in Hart territory. Amos has ignored William's requests for a meeting, so our alpha sent us here to take matters into our own hands. He has a message for Amos, and we want you to deliver it for us. Since Amos won't listen, we're hitting back where it hurts. Livestock. Family pets. Nothing is safe until that rogue is found."

Another low growl rumbled to his left, and Lucas glanced back at the wolf as it bared its red-stained teeth. He swallowed as the wolf stepped forward, its fangs inches from his face.

"George!" Bruce called, and the creature paused. "Let's go."

Bruce flashed a quick grin before he shifted, and the two werewolves sprinted into the woods, leaving Lucas alone and bleeding in the middle of the road.

SAM TOOK HIS TIME DESCENDING THE STAIRS. He turned the corner and drifted through the hallway toward the breakfast table. Amos probably wouldn't say anything about last night. Lucas was right. Their alpha hadn't brought up the fact that he didn't spend most nights in his own bed. But Amos would be within his rights to throw Sam out of the pack. After all, he was disobeying his alpha.

But would Amos really do that? It wouldn't be smart. Sam kept things running. Amos needed him.

Approaching the table, he kept his head low as he pulled his chair out and took a seat. He didn't need to look up to know Amos was watching him. The intensity of the alpha's stare burned into Sam's skin and made the hair on the back of his neck rise. He flitted his eyes toward Lucas's seat and was surprised to find his friend wasn't there.

"Where's Lucas?" Sam reached for the eggs as he threw the question out to no one in particular.

"I don't think he's come back from his run yet." Michael spoke around a mouthful of food. "Weird. He's usually back long before breakfast."

Sam's gaze wandered over to Roger, and he forced

an easy smile to try to erase the worried expression on Roger's face. "I'm sure he just decided to go a little farther than normal—"

The sound of the front door cut him off, and he called over his shoulder, "Did you decide to take the scenic route?" He started to laugh before he picked up the unmistakable scent of blood. Lots of it. He met Roger's eyes again, and the two of them rose from the table seconds before the rest of the pack followed suit.

A jolt of fear ran through Sam at the sight that greeted him at the front door. Lucas had managed to crawl inside, his bloodstained fingers leaving smudges on the marble floor. Sam reached Lucas seconds before his friend's arms gave out, and he propped Lucas up against the wall. A bruise was blossoming on his right cheek below a smattering of painful-looking road rash. More scrapes littered his arms under his torn shirt. Most alarming was the ugly, mangled mess on his left calf. Sam swallowed the bile that rose in his throat as he examined the blood and torn flesh.

Teeth marks.

"What the hell happened?" Sam grabbed a towel someone handed to him, and he wrapped it tightly around Lucas's leg as his friend hissed in pain.

"We got a visit from Bruce and George Cramer." Lucas clenched his jaw and groaned as Sam applied pressure to the deep wound. "Th-They brought a message from William for Amos."

"How long?"

The hostility in Michael's voice brought goose bumps to Sam's arms, and he cursed under his breath. The last thing they needed was for Michael to take off after the Cramers.

"It took me a while to get back here. Maybe ten minutes?"

Sam glanced up at Michael and wasn't surprised to see the yellow glow in his eyes.

Michael took a step toward the front door. "We can still catch them."

"No, Michael." Amos's voice came from down the hall. Their alpha stood back, away from everyone else, watching. Just his style. "I order you to stay put."

Michael ignored Amos and reached for the front door.

Sam clenched his fist. "Michael, no." When Michael froze at the sound of Sam's voice, Sam continued, "We can't go after them now. Not until we know what they want. Then we'll plan our next move. Please. Just stay put. We need you here."

With a frustrated growl, Michael turned on his heel and moved back toward the hallway. He clenched and unclenched his fists in anger, but he obeyed. He wouldn't go after the Cramers.

Satisfied that Michael wasn't going anywhere, Sam turned his attention back to Lucas. "Can you stand?"

Lucas nodded, grasping Sam's outstretched hand. Sam pulled him to his feet and did his best to steady Lucas as he wavered. His friend's pallor matched the white of the marble floor, and his limbs flopped like wet noodles. Sam took one of Lucas's arms while Roger took the other, and they half dragged, half carried Lucas to one of the couches in the living room. Lucas hissed in pain again as they lowered him onto the cushions, and Sam propped a pillow under his mangled leg. Sam peeled the towel away and gritted his teeth in sympathy.

"Daniel."

At Sam's word, Daniel appeared at his side.

"I think we can get away without taking him to the hospital, but this is going to need stitches."

Daniel nodded and wordlessly went toward the kitchen. Over the years, pack members had had their share of injuries. Falls...sprains...run-ins with wild animals. They tried to avoid the prying questions that came with visits to the hospital by patching up injuries at home when possible. Everyone learned first aid from a young age, but Daniel was the only one anyone trusted with stitches. Their first aid supplies included lidocaine, sutures, surgical needles and thread, and the good drugs.

Sam studied Lucas's face and smiled. "We'll get you something for the pain in just a minute. Okay, bud?"

Lucas nodded before his gaze drifted to a spot above Sam's head, and he swallowed thickly. Sam glanced over his shoulder and bit back a frustrated groan at the loathsome stare Amos aimed at Lucas.

"What's the message?" Amos spoke quietly and with no trace of emotion.

Sam growled under his breath. "Can't this wait, Amos?"

"No!"

The fury in Amos's gaze forced Sam to avert his eyes.

"What was the message?"

"Bruce said the rogue smells like one of the Harts. He said they'll be paying us back. Livestock. Family pets." Lucas swallowed again. "George was in wolf form. He was covered in blood. They've already killed. I could smell it."

"Amos..." Stuart spoke up from the other side of the room. "You know who is attacking livestock—"

"Enough!"

The venom in Amos's voice startled Sam, and he watched closely as Amos stalked across the room toward Stuart, his posture menacing. Sam rose, ready to intervene. Amos growled in warning, and Stuart snapped his mouth shut.

"I've had enough of you and your stories, old man."

Slowly, Stuart turned and shuffled across the floor toward the hallway. After he disappeared around the corner, Sam slid his gaze back to Amos. The tension in the air was palpable. Stuart knew something Amos clearly didn't want him to share with the rest of the pack. Who was Stuart talking about? No one had been gone from the pack house long enough to pull off the attacks in other territories. Sam eyed Amos. He needed to talk to Stuart when their alpha wasn't around. Something wasn't adding up.

"He was my baby!" Charlotte Moss hid her face in her hands, and the petite woman's shoulders shook as she sobbed.

"I know." Becca glanced around nervously at the lunch crowd she was supposed to be serving. Everyone stared as Becca comforted the distraught woman. She was just trying to be friendly when she'd asked Ms. Moss about her dog. How was she supposed to know? The woman had immediately dissolved into a puddle of tears as she relayed what happened to poor Marley between hiccupped sobs.

Becca had never owned any pets, but she knew how the English lit teacher felt about her beloved chocolate lab. She'd taken her class senior year and remembered the pictures of Marley that littered the teacher's desk. Ms. Moss always had a silly Marley anecdote to share with her students. Most of the kids rolled their eyes at the teacher's crazy obsession with her pooch, but Becca thought it was sweet.

"It just happened so fast. I let him out to do his business like I do every night. I heard a yelp, so I went out to look, and there was a giant wolf on top of him. I didn't know what to do, so I ran back into the house and called the police. By the time the sheriff got there, it was too late." Tears streamed down her face. "Oh, Becca, he was torn to shreds! There was nothing left of him." Another wail escaped the woman's throat as she bent over and buried her head in her hands.

Other stories of family pets that had been mauled had floated around in the last week. Becca knew of at least three. With those added to the cattle that had been killed out at the Baskin farm and the fresh deer carcasses that littered the sides of the roads outside town, people were in a panic.

"Ms. Moss, I'm going to bring you some ice cream. Extra chocolate topping. On the house." She rubbed Ms. Moss's back one last time and scurried off toward the kitchen. Guilt gnawed at her for leaving the woman alone, but she had other tables to tend to.

As she passed the bar, she caught a frown on Lucas's face as he looked toward Ms. Moss's table. She could almost swear a hint of guilt colored his expression. Maybe the scratches and bruises were skewing her perception. He'd brushed Becca off last week when she'd asked him about them and his very noticeable limp, mumbling about falling while he was out running. He didn't strike her as the clumsy type, but everyone tripped over their own feet sometimes.

Shaking her head, she hurried into the kitchen and asked for some ice cream for Ms. Moss then ran back out to the dining room to catch up on her tables. At least three were waiting to order. Damn Saturday lunch rush. Everyone wanted to get back outside to enjoy the weather, so she anticipated a few impatient grumbles, especially from the vacationers who didn't know Ms. Moss and cared nothing about her dog.

After taking a few orders and delivering some lunch specials, she nodded to a newly seated customer. Something in his gaze caused unease to settle in her stomach, but she smiled sweetly as she approached his table. "Hi there! My name is Becca, and I'll be taking your order. Can I start you out with something to drink?"

A thin smile snaked across the man's face. His neatly combed hair and freshly pressed clothes screamed sociopathic killer. Seconds ticked by as he gazed up at her quietly. Overall creepiness aside, something strangely familiar in his eyes pulled her in, and she found it hard not to stare. After almost twenty seconds passed without a word, she cleared her throat. "I guess you need another minute. I'll come back."

A shiver ran through her body as she turned and walked back toward table two, picking up an empty soda glass along the way. She glanced over her shoulder. Sure enough, the creepy man was still staring her way.

"Hey, Lucas, do you know the guy at table eight? I've never seen him before, and he doesn't look like your run-of-the-mill vaca—"

Becca stopped. Lucas's eyes had rounded, and his face paled as he stared at the man, whose creepy smile was still in place as he stared back at Lucas.

"Lucas? Do you know him?"

Finally, he turned to her. "How long has he been sitting there?"

"He just got here. You're freaking me out, Lucas. Who is he?"

A small, uneasy smile twitched at Lucas's lips. "It's nothing. That's Amos. He's one of Sam's cousins. He's just kind of an asshole. Hopefully, he'll be gone soon."

"Oh! That's why he looked familiar! It's the eyes."

Becca smiled. "If I had known he's related to Sam, I would have..." Becca looked back toward table eight. The man was gone. "That's weird. Where did he go?"

"Who knows. He probably has a puppy to kick somewhere." Lucas picked up a few empty beer bottles from the bar top and tossed them into the trash.

"Man, you really don't like him, do you? He's a Hart. How bad can he be?"

Lucas sighed. "Let's hope you never find out."

Every muscle in Lucas's body screamed in exhaustion as the Saturday-afternoon rush wound down. He grabbed a rag and started wiping up the condensation rings and spilled beer along the polished bar top. Ready for a break, he scanned the restaurant to gauge his timing. Would he be missed if he stepped out for a few minutes?

The door opened, and he watched a family enter from the boardwalk. Their sunburns, souvenir shirts, and insecure expressions screamed tourists. Wendy guided them into the dining room as their gazes scanned the area, taking in the variety of fish and wildlife mounted on the walls. The parents looked like squares. He doubted they would ask for anything the waitress couldn't handle. Sodas. Maybe a beer for good ol' dad.

"Lucas." His father's voice startled him, and he whipped his head toward the doorway as Roger made his way inside.

"Dad?" Lucas wracked his brain, trying to remember some reason his father might have for being in Miller's, where he rarely set foot, but he drew a blank. "What are you doing here?"

"I have something I need to talk to you about." Roger's tone struck Lucas as odd. Excited—but guarded. "Do you have a few minutes to talk?" He glanced around the room. "In private?"

"Your timing is good, actually," Lucas said. "I was just about to take a break."

With a glance around the dining room, he spotted Wendy flirting with one of the bus boys. Suppressing an eye roll, he called out to her. "Wendy!"

She straightened as though she'd been caught stealing and snapped her head toward Lucas.

He gave her a tight smile. "I'm taking a quick break. Be back in a few."

She bobbed her head in a nod then focused her attention back on the bus boy.

Lucas glanced at his father and shrugged, and they headed outside.

Vacationers filled the outdoor seating area, chatting, drinking, and soaking up the afternoon sun. All along the boardwalk, people milled about, talking and enjoying the lake view.

Roger pointed at the closest pier, and they crossed the boardwalk to the long wood-planked walkway that stretched over the water.

When they neared the end of the pier, Roger crossed his arms. "Have you given any more thought to what we've talked about?"

"You know I have," Lucas said quietly. "It's hard not to think about it. Have you heard anything more about Marcus?"

Roger shook his head. "That's what I came to talk to you about. Shawn said he's still in the hospital. They put him in a medically induced coma. His liver is failing."

Lucas's jaw went slack. "Do you think he'll die?"

"If we're lucky." Roger laughed.

"Dad!"

"Sorry." Roger waved a hand. "I know it's wrong to wish death on another person."

"But..." Lucas prompted his father.

"But...who knows." Roger peered out at the water for a moment before training his eyes back on Lucas. "Shawn talked to the Council. Because Marcus can no longer fulfill his duties as alpha, he's taking over. You know what that means. It's time, son. Shawn has said from the start that he doesn't want to be alpha. He's been grooming you. The pack is counting on you."

"Dad—"

"Just hear me out." Roger raised his voice, and Lucas quieted. "Shawn invited us to meet him at The Wild Boar. He just wants to talk." Roger lightly gripped Lucas's shoulder. "Whether or not you take over as alpha, he's going to invite us home, Lucas. You can finally see Beckett Falls."

Lucas's eyes rounded. He'd spent his entire life wishing to see Beckett Falls. His father told him stories, and he spent hours looking up pictures and reading about the town and the surrounding trails and scenic waterfalls. About the traditional Octoberfest the town was famous for celebrating each year. About the brewery.

Roger smiled as he studied Lucas's face. "What do you say? Are you ready to go home?"

TWENTY-SEVEN
BECCA

The sterile smells of the hospital burned Becca's nose when she stepped off the elevator onto the fourth floor. As she traveled the familiar path to Rosie's room, she reached into her bag for the shade of purple she'd brought for her friend's nails and smiled. Rosie would like the shade. Not too girly. A little edgy but not too out there.

As she pushed through the door to Rosie's room, Becca's breath caught in her throat. A man stood next to Rosie's bed. At first, she only saw his disheveled hair and rumpled clothes. When he turned around, she took a step back. That face. The same man she'd seen at table eight that morning stared back at her, but now his hair looked a little longer. Maybe it was just because it was messy. The rumpled T-shirt was a stark contrast to the pressed oxford he'd worn that morning.

Amos. Lucas had said his name was Amos.

"I'm sorry. I didn't mean to intrude." Becca stepped forward and extended her hand. "Amos? I believe I saw you this morning."

Amos narrowed his gaze before a small smile

played at his lips. He took a step toward her, and Becca took another one back. Creepy didn't begin to describe the vibe he put off. Instead of sociopathic serial killer, he screamed axe-wielding lunatic. No wonder Lucas didn't like him. If she had to live in a house with this man, she would never get a wink of sleep.

He said nothing as his eyes trailed up and down Becca's body. She crossed her arms self-consciously as his gaze lingered on her chest. He didn't even try to hide it. His gaze finally traveled back up to her face, and he smiled again as he drifted past her, out to the hall.

A shiver ran through her. The desire to run to her car and drive back to Hanks Hollow overcame her, but she'd come to see her friend. She wouldn't bail on Rosie.

Swallowing past the queasiness, she took a step forward and pulled a chair up next to Rosie's bed. "Hey, Rosie. How's it going? You have some interesting relatives, let me tell ya. I promised I would be back to paint your nails, so here I am."

"Becca?"

Becca turned at the sound of her name. Rosie's grandma, Clara, stood in the doorway, a baffled expression on her face. Clara's eyes darted around the room as though she were seeing something that wasn't there. "What's wrong?"

Just like Rosie, Clara seemed to be able to tell when something was off. Becca always figured they just had remarkable intuition, but it was a little alarming sometimes. "Oh, nothing. I was just a little spooked by Rosie's cousin. Don't tell Sam I said this, but he's kind of creepy."

"Creepy?" Clara wrinkled her brow. "Which cousin was it? Michael or Daniel?"

"Neither. It was Amos. I've actually never met him, but—"

"Amos was here?" Clara rushed forward and grabbed Rosie's hand. "How long ago?"

Confused by Clara's distress, Becca stumbled on her words. "H-He just left. Is everything okay?"

Clara didn't answer at first. She squeezed her eyes shut as she held Rosie's hand tightly. She seemed to be concentrating on something.

Becca let a few moments pass before she spoke again. "Clara?"

"Everything is fine." Clara opened her eyes and glanced at Becca. An awkward smile tilted the corner of her mouth as she placed Rosie's hand back down on the bed and patted it. "Just fine."

Becca watched Clara closely as the old woman grabbed another chair and sat down. "So, Becca, how have you been, sweetie?"

She let out a breath and smiled. "Really good, actually. I don't suppose you've heard..."

"About you and Sam? Oh yes. You're a hot topic. At least three of my clients have mentioned it." Clara rolled her eyes. "People love gossip."

Clara reached forward and took Becca's hand. The apprehension she'd felt seemed to melt away like magic. Clara's touch was so soothing, just like Rosie's. The old woman's eyes narrowed. "You're in love, aren't you? It pours out of you, darling."

Heat rushed to Becca's cheeks, and she smiled bashfully as she nodded. "I really am, Clara. I've never felt this way about anyone." Becca glanced at Rosie. "Do you think she would be okay with it?"

"Becca, I don't think you really need to ask that question, do you? You already know the answer."

She did. Rosie would never stand in the way of Becca's or Sam's happiness. She would celebrate their relationship as long as it made them happy.

Stepping quietly into Rosie's hospital room, Sam smiled as he watched Becca carefully paint his sister's nails. Clara gave him a sideways glance as he crept forward, sneaking up behind Becca. He moved his face close and gave her a quick peck on the cheek. She squealed and jumped in her chair, eliciting laughs from both Sam and Clara.

Becca huffed. "Sam, you made me smudge." She wiped at Rosie's fingers in frustration. "I want it to look perfect. This will be the longest-lasting manicure this girl has ever had."

Wrinkling his nose, Sam examined the purple fingernails. "Is it ethical to do that to her when she can't fight back?"

He dodged to the right as Becca swatted at him. "Shut up, Sam. It's a pretty color."

"If you say so."

"What are you doing here, anyway? I thought you usually come on Tuesdays." Becca puckered her lips.

Sam leaned down and kissed her. "Your dad told me you came up to visit, so I thought I would come and join you."

"Stalker."

Smiling, Sam shrugged. "Guilty."

"Speaking of stalker, I saw your cousin Amos twice today."

The smile dropped from Sam's lips. "What?"

"Yeah. He was at the restaurant, then he was here. It was weird. I've gone my whole life not knowing Amos Hart existed, then I saw him twice in one day."

His heartbeat thundering, Sam moved to the head of Rosie's bed. He studied his sister's face, reassuring himself that she was okay. Why would Amos be in Rosie's room? He ran his gaze over the machines surrounding the bed, trying to find anything that looked out of place. Had anything been unplugged? Turned off?

"Becca." Clara smiled as she reached into her pocket. "Would you please get me a soda? I need something sweet."

"Sure." Wrinkling her brow in confusion, Becca nodded as she took the change Clara handed to her, gave Sam a peck on the cheek, and went out to the hall.

When the door closed behind Becca, Clara turned to Sam. "She's okay, Sam. I had the nurses check everything out."

A weight lifted from his shoulders. "Thank you, Clara."

She shook her head. "It had me worried. That's for sure. I could feel a malevolent energy when I came into the room. He's no good, is he? I know you don't like him, but I never realized he was straight-up evil."

Evil? Maybe. Sam wondered what Amos was truly capable of. Would he kill Rosie if he had the chance? And what about Becca? He'd threatened to kill any girl who got knocked up, but would he kill

Becca just because Sam was dating her? Was he sending Sam a message? Letting him know he was aware of their relationship? Sam's stomach tightened.

"I don't want him here again, Sam. I don't want him near my granddaughter."

Clara's voice wavered, and Sam studied her. He'd never seen the woman shaken before.

"I don't want him here either, Clara." Sam bit his lip. "I'll talk to the guys. Maybe we can take up a rotation to make sure someone is always here."

"That would make me feel better." Clara squeezed Rosie's hand. "I've only been seeing clients two days a week so I can be here more, but I can cut it down to once a week. If you can have someone here every Tuesday, I'll cover all the other days."

Sam nodded. "I promise."

TWENTY-NINE
LUCAS

The Wild Boar—the tiny bar where Roger and Lucas had been meeting with the pack for years—looked the same as it had two years ago. Nothing changed, not even old Ethel, who greeted Lucas smelling of cigarettes and kitchen grease.

"So grown up," Ethel ground out in her raspy voice. "It's been such a long time, Lucas. You're skinny. Too skinny. You need a couple of burgers in you." She turned toward the kitchen and shouted to her husband. "Vern!"

"Already on it, Ethel," he yelled back. "Got a buncha burgers going."

"You boys sit down, and I'll bring you something to drink." Ethel wiped her hands on her apron and turned toward the bar, calling out over her shoulder, "If Shawn is coming to meet you, he'll want something from the beer-snob stock, I'm sure."

Lucas followed Roger to one of the rickety tables, and they sat in silence. Two old men sat at the bar, but otherwise, the place was empty.

"Is the whole pack coming, or is it just Shawn?" Lucas studied his fingers.

"Just Shawn."

A wave of disappointment hit him. Being at The Wild Boarbrought back a lot of fond memories, and he found himself missing his great-uncle Christopher and his cousin Travis almost as much as he missed his uncle Shawn. He'd pushed them out of his mind for so long. He'd pushed everything out of his mind.

"Sorry to keep you guys waiting." Shawn's voice snapped Lucas's attention to the door as his uncle stepped through. His tall frame commanded attention —all eyes were drawn his way. "Had some things to take care of in town before I headed down here. You been waiting long?"

Shawn covered the space between the door and their table in a few long strides, and he pulled a chair out then plopped down into it.

"Nah, we just got here a few minutes ago," Roger said. He leaned forward and gave his brother a one-armed hug, clapping him on the back. "It's good to see you, Shawn."

"It's good to see you guys too." Shawn leaned in and grasped Lucas's shoulder, giving him a little shake. "You've grown, kid." His eyes narrowed as he assessed Lucas. "You look older. And a little world-weary. You've been through some shit, huh?"

Lucas ducked his head. God, he didn't want this to turn into a therapy session.

"I'm sorry about what happened to you. And I'm really sorry about what happened to Rose."

Lucas flinched when Shawn said her name. Shawn didn't know her.

"I wouldn't wish anything bad to happen to you, but you got through it, kid, and it made you stronger."

Did it make him stronger? He didn't feel stronger. Far from it.

"Here you go, fellas." Ethel brought out three

plates of burgers and placed them on the table. "Let me just grab your beer."

"Better be Beckett's!" Shawn shouted after her.

Lucas picked at his burger as he watched Shawn and Roger douse their burgers with ketchup. Ethel returned a minute later with three bottles of Beckett's and put them on the table.

"Anything else, boys?"

"That'll do, Ethel." Shawn looked around. The two men at the bar had left, and they were alone. "Can we have the place for an hour?"

"Sure thing." Ethel turned and made her way to the front of the tavern. She flipped the sign on the window so that it read Closed and locked the door. "I'll be in the back if you need something."

"Thank you, Ethel," Shawn called.

Lucas took a bite of his burger as Shawn eyed him. "You've lost weight, kid. You need to beef up. Get some more muscle on you."

"He's looking much better than he did a few weeks ago." Roger spoke as though Lucas wasn't there, and Lucas rolled his eyes. "He had me worried for a while. He's been working at the bar in town. I think it's been good for him."

"That so?" Shawn grinned. "Giving them an education?"

"They needed it." Lucas said. "All they were serving was big-brand pilsner."

"That will keep their locals happy," Shawn said knowingly. "But Hanks Hollow is a tourist town. They need to keep up with the times."

"That's what I told them." Lucas grinned. "Charlie brought me on, and I pumped up their stock. The vacationers have been happy. Brought in a bunch of the nonalcoholic stuff too."

"You know, there's plenty of that in Beckett Falls." Shawn winked. "We have bars on every corner, selling Beckett's and other microbrews. The people there know their stuff, and they like to talk about it. You'll fit right in."

"Shawn, I'm not ready—"

"I didn't say anything about being alpha." Shawn pointed at Lucas. "Not yet. We'll talk about it, okay? I just want you guys to come back. Our pack is thin. There are only three of us and a pup, for Christ's sake. We need you guys."

Hope bubbled in Lucas's chest. He loved the Harts, but to be a part of the Beckett pack... To live in Beckett Falls...

"I want to talk about you taking over someday, Lucas." Shawn folded his hands in front of him. "I'm not going to pretend I'm not going to push you. I will. I really don't want to be alpha, kid. I belong out on the road, marketing our brand. And I still think you're the best man for the job. I haven't changed my mind about that. But we'll get you there when you're ready."

Lucas glanced at his father. He bit his lip when he saw the hope shining in his eyes. His father wanted to go home so badly that Lucas could practically smell the desire coming off him in waves.

What did they have left in Hanks Hollow? Amos ran the pack further into the ground every day. Living at Hart House sucked. He would miss Sam, Michael, and Daniel, but they would be fine without him.

The only thing really holding him there was Rosie, but she wasn't coming back. He had to face it sometime.

It was time to let go.

THIRTY

SAM

Sam watched the pendulum swing on the
enormous grandfather clock on the far wall of the
dining room. The *ticktock* swallowed the silence in
the room. It had to be pretty quiet for a ticking clock
to sound too loud. He'd forgotten how morose the
pack dinners had become. The first meal he'd shared
with them in weeks felt like penance for some crime
he didn't realize he'd committed. God, why had he
decided to eat dinner here? He should have been enjoying a burger with Becca at Miller's.

His gaze drifted across the table to Stuart. The
old man picked at his food, seemingly oblivious to the
suffering of his grandsons who sat on either side of
him. Michael looked like he wanted to blow his brains
out, and Daniel had been drawing pictures in his
mashed potatoes for the past five minutes.

It had been easy to ask Michael and Daniel to
start taking rotations with him at the hospital. A quick
text to each of them, and they'd responded almost immediately. They would do anything for Rosie.

Now he just needed five minutes alone with his
great uncle. Stuart didn't have a cell phone, and even

if he did, the old man wouldn't begin to know how to use it. Sam needed to find a way to talk to him, though. He wanted to know what secret Stuart was holding on to. What did Amos not want the rest of the pack to know?

His gaze drifted to Amos. Smug, arrogant asshole.

The alpha ate his food slowly, barely sparing a glance at his pack. He insisted no one was to take a bite before him at dinner, and no one was to leave the table until he was finished. It was a werewolf thing. In wolf form, alpha werewolves always ate before the rest of the pack when they hunted in the woods, but to enforce it at the dinner table while they were in human form was just ridiculous. They'd never done it under Simon's leadership. Simon had never needed to create dumb rules to show dominance.

And what the hell was he doing in Rosie's hospital room? And at Miller's? He was up to something. Sam was almost sure of it. Anxiety made his stomach churn.

Amos seemed to sense Sam was staring at him, as his gaze flitted in his direction. He narrowed his eyes. "Sam. Stop that tapping."

Huh? Sam looked down at his hands. He didn't realize he'd started hitting his fork against his plate to the tune of the *ticktock* of the clock. He took a deep breath in through his nose. "So. What's everyone doing tonight?"

As he gazed around the room, his question was met with a sea of blank stares. He turned back to Amos. The alpha chewed his food slowly and narrowed his eyes at Sam.

"Stuart, are you up for a game of euchre tonight? I'm sure Daniel and Michael will play." Sam smiled at

Stuart. Amos wouldn't want anything to do with their card game. It would be the perfect opportunity to talk to Stuart.

Surprise flickered across Stuart's face then a flash of alarm as he glanced toward Amos. Sam followed his gaze, and his stomach tightened at the glare their alpha fixed on Stuart.

Stuart swallowed before he lowered his eyes to his plate. "Maybe another time, Sam. I think I'll head to bed early tonight."

Sam gritted his teeth in anger at the smug expression on the alpha's face. Stuart was afraid, and it didn't take a genius to know why. What had Amos threatened him with?

When the excruciatingly boring dinner was over, Sam went to his room. He lay back on his bed and stared up at the ceiling, wishing he was at Becca's. His mind strayed to Lucas. Michael said he and Roger had booked one of the cabins and were doing some fishing. They used to have father–son days long ago, before the attack. Maybe they'd started them again. Something didn't seem right about it, though.

Suddenly, a scream and a series of loud crashes echoed through the hallway. Sam shot to his feet, whipped his bedroom door open, and ran toward the stairs, the source of the noise. As he turned the corner, he almost collided with Amos. The alpha stood on the top step, staring down the staircase. A strange smile adorned his lips.

Sam followed Amos's gaze, and his heart leaped to his throat. "Stuart!"

He half ran, half stumbled down the stairs to his great uncle. Stuart lay in a heap, his head and arms splayed across the floor and his legs twisted on the bottom few stairs. As Sam reached his side, he touched the man's shoulder, but he paused. He didn't dare move him. His neck could be broken. Blood marred the top of Stuart's head where it had collided with the marble floor. His limbs contorted in awkward angles, obviously broken.

His breath catching in his throat, Sam looked back up the stairs to where Amos was still standing, the sinister smile still plastered on his face.

"He fell." Amos sounded as though he was commenting on the weather. "I tried to catch him, but I just wasn't fast enough."

"Call 911!" Sam's voice shook as he shouted the order at Amos. He would deal with the repercussions of speaking to his alpha that way later.

When he turned back to Stuart, his stomach clenched. Behind him, he heard the rumble of running feet.

"Grandpa! No!" The anguish in Daniel's voice was heartbreaking as he tumbled to Stuart's side.

"Don't move him, Daniel," Sam ordered. He turned back to Amos. Of course, the alpha hadn't moved. He hadn't called for help. "I'm going to get my phone from my room so I can call for help. We'll get him to a hospital, Daniel."

Sam squeezed Daniel's shoulder as he bolted up the stairs toward his room and his phone. As he passed by Amos, he could have sworn he heard a giggle.

"I came as soon as my shift was over," Becca said as she breezed down the hospital corridor toward the small waiting area outside the ICU.

Sam was surprised to see her, but he was glad she was there. He stood to greet her, and she gave him a tight hug. Her arms felt good wrapped around him, and he breathed in her perfume.

Next to him, Martha cleared her throat in a not-so-subtle way. Michael, Daniel, and Lucas were well aware of Sam's relationship with Becca, but he had left the rest of the house in the dark. Long-term relationships weren't the norm in their world, and he wasn't really sure how it would be received.

"Rebecca," Sam said, giving an uncomfortable little cough. "This is Martha. She is our—"

"I raised this boy," Martha said, getting to her feet. "I've been waiting to meet you for some time."

Sam scrunched his face in confusion, and Martha gave a hearty laugh.

"Oh, please, Sam," she said, slapping his shoulder. "I knew you had a girlfriend as soon as you started wearing cologne and clean underwear every day. Don't forget who does your laundry."

Sam's cheeks heated, and he looked for the closest window he could jump through.

"Oh my God." Becca smothered a laugh with her hand before she extended the other to Martha. "It's really nice to meet you."

They shook hands and started talking, each of them going a mile a minute. The two most talkative people in the world were in a room together. No one else would get a word in edgewise.

Becca took Sam's hand and planted herself in the chair next to the one he had been sitting in as she continued talking with Martha. She pulled him down so that he was sitting next to her. Her hand slid down to his knee, and she squeezed it reassuringly.

"So, how is he doing?"

Sam realized that he was suddenly being pulled into the conversation with Becca's question.

Sam shook his head sadly. "Not well. Michael and Daniel are saying goodbye."

"Oh my God!" Her hands flew to her mouth, then she threw her arms around Sam's neck in a hug. "I'm so sorry, Sammy."

Sam closed his eyes and melted into her embrace. When he opened his eyes again, Amos was standing in front of them. He glared at Sam, his lip curled up in anger. Sam flinched and stood quickly, nearly knocking Becca to the floor.

"Amos, what are you doing here?"

"I'm here for Stuart," Amos said, his eyes on Becca.

It was the obvious answer, and it made Sam's question sound stupid, but he had never expected Amos to come.

Amos's eyes ran over Becca. "Get rid of her."

Becca gasped, and he had to fight the urge to punch Amos.

Sam turned to her and put a hand on her shoulder. "I'm sorry, Becca," he said nervously. "He's kind of rude. He just means that it would be better if you waited for me at home. We better keep it to family right now."

Becca reddened as she tucked in her chin bashfully, and Sam felt like an ass.

"Oh my gosh, you're right. I'm so sorry. I'm intruding."

She gathered her purse and gave Sam a peck on the cheek before she rushed out. Sam watched her leave, wanting so badly to follow her.

Amos gave Sam a murderous glare. "I warned you about this, pup."

Sam stepped forward, his fists clenched.

A noise came from behind him, and he turned to see his cousin. A single tear dripped down Daniel's cheek.

"He's gone."

A warm breeze tickled Lucas's arm as he rested it on the open window frame of his truck. He stared across the parking lot at the brick building that had eluded him for so long. It looked like a typical hospital. He had never been afraid of them before, and he wasn't particularly afraid of this one.

He was just scared to face one of the patients inside.

He'd lost count of the number of times he'd made the drive here, where he would sit, staring up at the building for hours before he lost his nerve and went home. He couldn't bear to see her confined to a hospital bed, buried in medical equipment and smelling like sterilization liquid. Rosie brought life to everything she touched. That was how he wanted to remember her. That was how he would always remember her.

When he'd heard about Stuart, he wanted to come and be there for the man who'd been like a grandfather to him. To be there for the rest of the pack. Sam had said Stuart wouldn't live much longer, but Lucas just couldn't bring himself to walk through those doors.

He'd hoped maybe he could get himself to step inside. To say goodbye to Stuart. To say goodbye to...

No. He couldn't say goodbye to her. He just couldn't.

On the seat next to him, his phone buzzed. He sighed, taking one last look at the hospital before he started the truck's engine. He picked up the phone from his seat without glancing at the caller ID.

"Hey."

Lucas was surprised to hear Sam's voice.

"Hey, Sam." Lucas swallowed. "How's Stuart?"

After a long pause, Sam spoke softly. "He just passed, Lucas. I'm sorry."

Lucas rested his head on the steering wheel and closed his eyes. His mind went to the days he'd spent watching Stuart read to Rosie. She would have been crushed to hear about this.

"You okay, buddy?" Sam's voice on the other end of the line snapped Lucas out of his thoughts.

"I'm okay, Sam. How are you holding up?"

"I'll be fine. Daniel is a wreck. Michael is Michael. It's hard to tell with him sometimes."

"Yeah," Lucas said. "I'll see you all back at the house tonight?"

"Yeah." Sam paused. "See you later, Lucas."

Lucas ended the call and bit his lip. He took one last look up at the hospital and swallowed the lump that had formed in his throat. Leaving without saying goodbye was wrong. She deserved better. But he put his truck into gear and drove out of the parking lot.

Once again, Lucas had failed Rosie.

The Hart family had a cemetery about half a mile from the house, where all the Hart family ancestors were buried. Walking through the cemetery felt like walking back through time. The dates etched on the old, crumbling tombstones became older and older as the cemetery stretched on.

Sam stood at his father's plot and stared down at the gravestone, thinking about the day of his funeral. Nearly the entire town had come. It had driven Amos nuts to have that many people at the Hart estate.

Not many people had been at Stuart's funeral. He didn't really have any acquaintances outside the pack. It was a nice service. The pastor from one of the churches in Hanks Hollow officiated. Stuart wasn't a religious man, but he would have liked it.

Daniel and Michael stood next to the spot where the casket had been lowered into the ground only half an hour ago. Each appeared lost in thought. Stuart and Michael had never been that close. But Michael and Jack had been inseparable, and Jack's death had torn Michael apart. Unlike Jack, Stuart had always been quiet and kept to himself. He and Daniel were a lot alike in that way, and their bond had grown closer over the past year or so. Stuart had been teaching Daniel how pack records were kept in the library, and Daniel had been slowly taking over the task.

"Are you okay, Sammy?"

Sam turned to Becca. She had insisted on coming to support him, and he didn't have the heart to tell her not to. He knew Amos would get on him about it, but he didn't care.

"Yeah, I'm okay. I just wanted to say hello to my father as long as I'm here."

Becca smiled and took his hand. He could feel Amos staring at them, and for a moment, Sam felt a thrill of fear travel up his spine. He was putting her in even more danger.

He squeezed Becca's hand, wanting to keep her close. "Let's get out of here."

~

"Charlie! How about another round of shots!"

Michael propped his feet on the table and tipped his chair back until it was teetering on the back legs. Sam waited for him to fall. It wouldn't be the first time. They had come straight from the funeral, so Michael was still dressed in his suit. His jacket had been discarded, and his tie was loosened around his neck. He had his sleeves rolled up to his elbows.

"You got it, Mikey," Charlie called.

Normally, Charlie would have had some back-handed comment about Michael yelling to him across the bar, but he was being gentle tonight. Sam watched him grab a handful of shot glasses and some of the good whiskey from under the bar. He lined the glasses up and started pouring.

The last thing Sam wanted was more to drink,

but Michael wouldn't be happy unless they were all drowning their sorrows with him. Sam put his arm around Becca and pulled her closer to him. The alcohol made him frisky and uninhibited. He kissed her passionately, running his fingers over her soft cheeks.

"U-uh," Charlie chided them as he strolled over to the table with a tray full of shots. He put the tray down as he smacked the back of Sam's head. "Keep that stuff out of my sight. I'm happy you're dating my daughter, but you don't have to flaunt it."

"None of us want to see that, Sam," Michael whined.

Daniel laughed and hiccupped. He was almost as reserved as a drunk as he was sober. Instead of just sitting silently in the chair, he was sitting silently in the chair with a goofy grin.

"Lucas!" Michael called out. "Stop brooding in the corner like a pansy and come over here to do a shot with us."

Distant the last few days, Lucas was sitting by himself. Something was bugging him. It was more than the loss of Stuart. Something seemed to be weighing heavily on him. Sam promised himself he would talk with him tomorrow.

"Jeez, Michael," Becca whispered as she rubbed her head.

Lucas mumbled something before he stood and walked over to the table. He wore an angry scowl, but he wouldn't say anything to Michael. Not tonight.

"Nice of you to join us, son." Roger scowled at Lucas.

Sam had almost forgotten that Roger was sitting there. He didn't usually join them when they went out.

"To my grandpa," Daniel said, raising his shot glass.

Daniel's lower lip dropped, like he was going to say more, but he stopped. He teared up, and his Adam's apple bobbed as he gulped.

Sam picked up his shot glass and held it up. "To Stuart."

Everyone raised their glasses in unison, cheering Stuart, then downed their drinks.

"Hey, hey, hey, the gang's all here," Roger said, nodding toward the door with a frown.

Sam almost choked on his whiskey as he watched Amos come into the bar wearing that awful, conceited grin. He strolled toward the table and ran his eyes over each member of the pack.

"Don't stop the celebration on my account," he said. "I just came to say hello."

Sam was cozied up with Becca, and Amos stared daggers at them. Becca's body tensed. Sam untangled himself from her and stood.

"Amos, I didn't expect to see you here," he said.

"Clearly." His eyes flicked to Becca. "I thought I told you to—"

"We were just leaving."

Sam didn't want Amos to finish his sentence with both Becca and Charlie in the room. He had already hurt Becca's feelings once. If he repeated those words in Charlie's presence, Charlie would kick Amos out on his ass. As much as Sam would love to see that, it was best not to let it get that far.

Sam took Becca's hand and pulled her to her feet. She looked confused and a little bit angry.

"We were having a good time," Becca whispered. "I don't want to leave yet."

Sam sighed and glanced at Amos. He'd found an

empty chair and made himself comfortable. Everyone else had grown tense. The atmosphere no longer felt relaxed and friendly.

"What can I get for you, friend?" Charlie asked Amos.

"Charlie…" Sam hesitated, feeling very uncomfortable. "This is Amos. He's my father's cousin."

"Ah! Simon was a good man," Charlie said, extending his hand. "He's sorely missed around here."

Amos stared at Charlie but didn't shake his hand.

"I'll take a glass of whiskey, *friend*," Amos said, the conceited grin still plastered on his face.

Charlie glanced at Sam, and Sam shrugged and rolled his eyes. His heart was beating fast. He wanted to know what Amos was doing here. If it were anyone else, he would say he was joining them in their celebration of Stuart's life, but he knew better. That wasn't Amos's style.

"It's nice to see you here, Amos," Becca said, sitting back down. She giggled. "Your family keeps us in business."

When Amos didn't laugh with her, she cleared her throat uncomfortably.

"It seems this has become quite the hot spot for my family." Amos flitted his gaze around the table. "The house gets lonely without them around. I guess if I want to keep tabs on them, I'll have to come around here a little more often."

Becca grinned. "Well, good! I'm glad we'll be seeing more of you."

Sam glanced at Michael and Daniel. They remained quiet and stone-faced. Amos's presence appeared to have sobered them up.

"I'm really tired, Becca," Sam said. "I think we should go."

The need to get her out of there became more overwhelming with each moment.

"Remember what I told you, Sam," Amos said. "Watch it."

Becca didn't argue when Sam took her hand and led her toward the door, yelling a thank-you to Charlie.

"Okay." Becca sounded angrier than he had ever heard her as they walked out of the bar. She took her keys out and unlocked her door as she shook her head. "What the hell was that?"

"Amos is an ass," Sam said as they climbed the stairs to her apartment. "No one likes him."

"No. It was more than that." Becca threw her keys onto the end table as they walked into the living room then plopped down on the couch and stared at him. "You were all weird around him. Like you were afraid of him."

"It's complicated," Sam said carefully. "Our relationship with him is—"

"Complicated? Really?" Becca tilted her head in disbelief.

"I think it's best if you stay away from him. Or at least it's best if we stay away from each other when he's around."

"Are you being serious right now? Do you realize how weird and messed up that sounds?"

Sam sighed and sat down next to her. The room spun, and he cursed Michael for pushing that last shot. How could he possibly explain to Becca why Amos was dangerous? He hated lying to her. It came so easy with other girls but not with her. Not just because she could see right through him but because he didn't *want* to lie to her. He wanted her in his life, and being a werewolf was a big part of that. Damn the

Council and their stupid laws. Maybe the alcohol made him a little braver. Or dumber.

Nodding, his mind made up, he took a deep breath and steeled himself for the conversation ahead.

"Becca, there's something I need to tell you."

Becca stared at the wall. A small crack stretched about a foot down from the ceiling. She concentrated on the random flaw, letting the distraction calm her. Anything to avoid the conversation Sam was trying to have with her. Because one of two things had become real tonight. Either Sam was out of his ever-loving mind, or his entire family—including Rosie—was a bunch of werewolves. *And* Rosie was a witch.

It seemed so much easier to believe Sam was crazy, but the pieces fit. They fit so damn well. All these years, she'd known they were all different. She knew Rosie was special.

But never, not in her wildest dreams, did she ever imagine it was *this*.

"Say something. Please," Sam said for the hundredth time.

Becca opened her mouth, but words wouldn't form. What do you say to that? What do you say when your boyfriend tells you he's a werewolf? There was no article in *Vogue* to cover this.

"I..." Becca's throat went dry.

"You know I would have told you a long time ago

if I could have. And you know Rosie wanted to tell you a million times when she was young. I can't tell you how many times I heard her beg my dad to let her tell you."

A lump formed in Becca's throat, and tears welled in her eyes. The whiskey shots from earlier wanted to make a reappearance. Sam promised they weren't dangerous werewolves. They didn't hunt humans. At least not *anymore*. What the hell did that mean?

"You have to believe me, Becca, please." Sam scrubbed a hand over his face. "Most of us aren't much different from your typical human, okay? But we used to be. Werewolves used to be dangerous. They captured women and..." Sam swallowed. "Did awful things to them."

Becca didn't think she wanted to know what awful things he was talking about.

"Most of us don't do that anymore, but there are some, like Amos, who want to go back to the old way of doing things. That's why he's dangerous. That's why I need you to stay away from him."

"A-And that's why you don't want him to see us t-together?" Becca finally found her voice, and she kicked herself for the stutter that came out. "You think he'll hurt me?"

"I won't let him." Sam set his jaw.

"This is too much." A tear slid down her cheek. "I don't know what to do with this."

"I know. It's a lot." Sam ran a hand through his curls, making them stand straight up. "Jesus, I should have thought this through. No wonder telling humans is outlawed."

"So you're breaking the law now?"

"I'm not supposed to be telling you."

"What happens if they find out you told me?"

Becca's mind went to the freaky council-wolfy-people Sam had described. They didn't sound like anyone she wanted to meet.

Sam's silence sent a spike of fear through Becca's body, and she repeated her question angrily. "Sam, what happens if they find out you told me?"

"They'll kill you."

"Jesus, Sam!"

"I'm not planning to tell anyone. Unless you plan to, it's okay." Sam sighed. "I thought you should know. I didn't want to keep this from you anymore. But I picked the wrong time to tell you. This was dumb. I shouldn't have—"

"I need you to get out of here." Becca's knees went weak as she stood. Sam reached a hand out to steady her, but she slapped it away. "Don't touch me. I need to be alone. I need to think. You need to leave."

"Can we just talk about this? Please?" Sam's beautiful brown eyes glistened with tears, and Becca almost forgot why she was angry.

God, why did he have to look like such a sad, sweet puppy dog? Puppy...wolf...oh God, he *was* a puppy dog.

"I just need to be alone, Sam." Becca's voice wavered. "Go home. We'll talk tomorrow."

Sam ducked his head and nodded before he turned and walked to the door. He hesitated before he opened it then closed it behind him.

Letting out a shaky sigh, Becca started to pace the living room. She shook her hands. Restless energy vibrated through her body. She needed to get out and take a walk. She grabbed her hoodie from the back of the couch and pulled it on before heading for the door.

Becca sniffed and wiped at her eyes as her heels clicked along the boardwalk. She examined the smudges of mascara on her fingers and imagined the mess her face must look. The wind picked up off the water, and she hugged her hoodie a little more tightly to her body. She still wore her little black dress from the funeral, and the late-night cold bit at her bare legs.

She paused to stare out at the lake. The overhead lights on the boardwalk only stretched so far, then the blackness of night swallowed everything. She could just make out the outline of the trees on the bluffs under the faint moonlight that peeked through the clouds. That creepy darkness...

"Lots of forest out there."

Becca's heart leaped to her throat, and she spun on her heel to face the stranger behind her. Only it wasn't a stranger.

"Amos!" she screeched.

"People get lost in those woods all the time." Amos took a step forward, studying Becca's face, before he cast his gaze out toward the bluffs. "Someone could disappear out there, and no one would ever find them."

Her heart thundered as her breath shuddered. Every instinct told her to run, but her feet stayed frozen to the boardwalk. Her heels might as well have been embedded into the wood.

"He told you, didn't he?" Amos studied her face again. "I can smell your fear."

"W-W-What do you mean?" Becca could barely rasp out the words. No way he believed her. She didn't sound convincing to her own ears.

"You know this means I'll have to kill you, right?"

Her knees weakened, and she braced herself against the wood railing. Glancing over her shoulder, she briefly contemplated jumping into the water. It wasn't a long drop. Maybe...

A sound came from close to her ear. She turned her head just in time to see a fist soaring toward her face, then the world went dark.

THIRTY-FOUR
LUCAS

"We'll need to leave our phones behind." Roger spoke softly as he helped Lucas pack the last of his clothes in his duffle bag.

The sun just barely lit the sky. The quiet of the house made Lucas's ears ring.

"What? Why?" He counted on his phone as a lifeline to everyone he knew.

"We're on their phone plan, Lucas." Roger sighed. "It's best we cut all ties. Leave our phone numbers, phones, vehicles—everything they gave us."

"How are we going to get there if we leave our vehicles?" Lucas scowled. "So what? We'll have nothing but the clothes on our backs?"

"Simon paid me a salary while he was alive. I have a lot of money put away, and I bought a car with cash. It's outside." Roger zipped Lucas's duffle closed and slung it over his shoulder. "The Beckett pack will provide us with everything we need, Lucas."

"Just like the Harts did." Lucas frowned. He'd always felt like a guest in Hart House. Would he feel that way in Beckett House too? When would he have a place that felt like his home and not just somewhere he stayed?

He dug his phone out of his pocket and held it for a moment. It contained a lot of saved text conversations he would miss. Love notes from Rosie. He took a deep breath before he placed it carefully on top of the dresser.

Time to let go.

He intended to message Sam after they got there, but he would just have to send one when he got his own phone. Maybe Shawn had a laptop he could borrow. He could email him. Sam checked his email sometimes.

Roger had hounded Lucas to stay quiet about everything. He didn't want anyone knowing anything until after they'd left. They couldn't risk word getting back to Amos. The alpha could punish them for deserting the pack. Once they were accepted into the Beckett pack, they would have their protection.

It felt dirty to use Stuart's death as a distraction, but everyone would be hungover this morning. Not likely to hear the commotion of them packing their stuff and leaving. Michael's snores punctuated the silence now and again, but otherwise, the house remained quiet. Too quiet. Lucas hated leaving it like this. He wanted to remember it how it used to be. Loud, fun, happy.

The sun barely peeked over the treetops when Lucas and Roger climbed into Roger's new car. After they buckled in, they sat in silence for a moment before Roger cleared his throat and started the engine. Lucas couldn't help turning to look over his shoulder at Hart House as the car coasted down the driveway. The enormous house seemed to shrink as they drove farther away.

"Don't worry about what's back there, Lucas."

Roger focused on the road. "Keep your eyes forward. You've got a bright future ahead of you, son."

Lucas eyed his father for a moment before he turned his gaze to the road as well. As they drove east toward Beckett territory, he had the perfect view of a glorious rising sun.

THIRTY-FIVE

ROSIE

The nervous energy of the rabbit hit Rosie
long before she spotted the little animal camouflaged
against the trunk of a tree. She shuffled her feet, and it
froze. A wave of its fear washed over her.

"Show him he shouldn't be afraid of you." Gwen's
voice behind her was soft and encouraging.

Rosie concentrated. The rabbit's little nostrils
flared quickly then receded as she sent a soothing energy out to him. His response was immediate. He
calmed, letting down his guard and twitching his ear
as he took a few steps toward Rosie.

Something nearby caught Rosie off guard. Anticipation. Hunger. She scrunched her face in sympathy
for the rabbit as her eyes flitted to a spot behind the
little creature. A bobcat inched forward, crouched
low to the ground, partially concealed by a fern. As it
stalked the rabbit, its hunting instincts gave off an
anxious energy that made a knot form in Rosie's stomach. She knew that feeling well. Every time she
hunted with the pack, she felt that primal urge.

No. The rabbit wouldn't have been caught off
guard if she hadn't calmed him. She shifted her energy to the bobcat, willing it away. The cat's paw

froze in midair, and it relaxed its body before backing off and shaking its head. It glanced at Rosie for a moment before it took off through the forest.

"Good, Rosie!" Her mother put a hand on her shoulder. "You're getting really good at this."

The warmth of her mother's love ran through Rosie as she turned to face her. She grinned at her proud smile. "I know you said Grandma doesn't have this kind of magic. Do you?"

Her mother shook her head. "Not nearly this strong. The gods have blessed you."

Heat rushed to her cheeks as anxiety gnawed at her stomach.

"I can feel your worry, Rosie." She squeezed Rosie's hand. "Just concentrate on putting one foot in front of the other. Don't worry about the future. What will be will be."

"What if I do the wrong thing? I don't know what they want me to do."

"Shh." Gwen brushed her hands through Rosie's hair, and she placed a gentle kiss on her temple. "Don't worry about that. They have a plan for you. It will all play out as it's supposed to. Trust your instincts." She placed a hand on Rosie's chest. "Trust your heart, Rosie. I know it's a good one."

With her mother's touch, the worry left Rosie. She closed her eyes and took a deep breath. Spending time with her mother was something that only ever happened in her dreams. Maybe this was a dream, too, but she didn't care. It felt real, and it was better than she could ever have imagined.

"Our time is almost up."

Rosie's stomach tightened, and her eyes stung with tears. "No. Not yet. Please."

"You're going to do great things."

"How do you know that?"

"You're already doing great things, Rosie. Just keep being you."

A familiar voice behind Rosie startled her, and she spun around.

"She's amazing, isn't she?" Her father smiled at her, and his gaze shifted to Gwen. "We did good."

"Daddy?" She rushed forward and leaped into his arms. His solid chest and warm embrace were safe and secure, his love and support as strong and un-yielding as the oak tree.

He stroked the top of Rosie's head, as he'd done so many times before, and she melted further into his arms. When she finally forced herself to step back, she studied his face. Gone were the worry lines that had always creased his forehead. Years as pack alpha had weighed heavily on him. Now, he looked peace-ful. Happy. He brushed a hand over Rosie's cheek, wiping away a tear, and he smiled.

"Always be you, Rosie. You're perfect." His soft voice touched her heart and made it swell. He shifted his gaze to Gwen again. "Are you ready?"

Her mother stepped forward, and the two of them stared into each other's eyes for what felt like an eter-nity before they leaned into each other. Rosie almost averted her gaze as they kissed—the moment seemed so intimate—but the tenderness in their closeness drew her in.

The love that radiated from them as they em-braced was like nothing she'd ever felt before, and her jaw went slack as a flaming aura engulfed them. She knew that flame. She felt it inside her.

She faltered for a moment before she spoke. "Mates?"

Her mother turned toward her. "The love that

draws us together transcends this world. I suppose you could call it mates."

"Like…" Her eyes darted to her father then to the ground, and her cheeks heated.

"Like what you and Lucas have." Her father's voice drew her back to him, and she studied his smile. No anger or disappointment or overprotective fatherly chastising. Just a genuine smile.

"He needs you, Rosie." Her mother reached for her father's hand. Something in the air shifted. They were saying goodbye. "Soon, you'll be able to return to him."

"But I still don't know what I'm supposed to do!" Rosie's panic rose from her stomach to her chest.

"Just keep being you, Rosie," her father said. "Just look what effect you've had on our pack."

"What do you mean?" Rosie furrowed her brow.

Gwen nodded toward a spot behind Rosie. "You have a visitor."

She didn't want to turn around. People seemed to disappear when she did that. Still, the feeling of being watched forced her to turn her head. In the distance, a man stood in the shadow of the trees.

A soft breeze blew, and she turned back just in time to watch as her parents walked into the forest, hand in hand. Their bodies slowly vanished as they stepped into the trees.

"Rosie?"

The familiar weary voice startled her, and she spun on her heel as he stepped closer, into the light.

A tear dripped down her cheek as she gasped. "Stuart?"

Pain seared through Becca's skull. A headache didn't begin to describe it. She tried to make sense of her muddied memories but failed, so she focused on the present. Her cheek rested against a hard floor. That couldn't be right. She moved her limbs. Everything hurt. When she placed her palm against the ground, the cold seeped into her skin.

Opening her eyes to a slit, she flicked her gaze around the room. Concrete floor. Steel bars. Prison? Was she in jail? No. It wasn't a police station. She propped herself up on her hands, and her head spun as she got a better look at her surroundings. Small windows lined the top of the opposite wall. A basement? A cell in a basement?

Fear crawled up her skin as memories of the night before flooded her brain. Sam. Werewolf. Amos.

"Ow." She touched the side of her head where pain blossomed. A tender area on her cheek felt swollen.

"That will hurt for a while" came a voice to her left.

Becca turned toward it. Amos appeared in a doorway in the outer part of the room. There were two cells, hers and an empty one. Otherwise, the room was bare.

"Where am I?" Becca's voice shook, from the cold or fear or both, she wasn't sure.

"You're at Hart House." Amos smiled. "Bet Rose never showed you the basement when you came to visit."

"No," Becca whispered. "She didn't."

Becca had only visited Hart House a few times when she was young. Rosie's father rarely let her have visitors. On the few occasions Becca visited, they spent most of their time in Rosie's room. Becca had always wanted to explore the rest of the enormous house, but Simon was weird about it.

"The basement is the only part of the house that's stayed the same since our ancestors settled here. The rest of the house has been rebuilt and remodeled several times." Amos stepped forward and gazed at the bars of the cell. "Lots of history down here. It's where all the older members of the pack were born. Sam's father was born right there in that very spot you're sitting."

Becca's stomach somersaulted, and she held her breath.

"Aren't you going to ask what happened to Simon's mother?" His gaze narrowed as he ran a hand up the bars.

Becca couldn't find her voice, so she just shook her head. She didn't want to hear it. She didn't want to know.

"The pack ate her." His eyes lit with excitement. "It was before my time. We haven't had another down here since then. I never got to see the ritual done. The alphas of my time wouldn't allow it."

Becca's body shook. Her breath hitched, and tears blurred her vision.

Amos stepped closer, practically pressing his face against the bars. For a moment, she was thankful for the cell door that separated her from the monster staring down at her. "I'm alpha now. And I think it's time to bring the ritual back."

Becca's heart dropped into her stomach, and her mind went blank as she started screaming.

SAM DIDN'T GET A WINK OF SLEEP. AS THE alcohol wore off from the night before, the sheer stupidity of what he'd done drove deeper into his brain, like an icepick. It left a searing, pounding pain that was amplified by his hangover.

He'd scared her away and put her in danger. What was wrong with him?

Still, the anger mingled with relief. No more hiding. He could be himself. Completely himself. No secrets. No holding back. He didn't want to hold back with Becca. He wanted to give her every part of him. The good and the bad. He prayed she would come to terms with the bad eventually.

If she didn't...

His phone buzzed somewhere among the mess of pillows and blankets, and he tore through the sheets until he found the device. He tensed with hope. The caller ID read Charlie's name, and Sam frowned. He looked at the time. 9:00 a.m.

"Charlie?" He tried to keep the drowsy fog from his voice.

"Are you with Becca? She was supposed to be here at eight to help me with inventory. It's not like her to not show. I know you guys had a bit to drink last night, but you tell her that's no excuse to sleep late and ignore my phone calls—"

"Charlie, I'm at my place. I didn't stay with her last night." Sam bit his lip, worry inching its way up his spine. "I'll try to get in touch with her. Maybe she just overslept. If she doesn't pick up, I'll drop by."

"Don't bother, Sam." Charlie sounded irritated. "I've still got a key. I'll go up there and haul her ass out of bed."

"Don't be too hard on her," Sam said. "We were up late, talking. Really, she probably just forgot to set an alarm."

Sam's sensitive hearing picked up something, and he tilted his head to the side. Was that a scream? "I have to go, Charlie. I'll call you as soon as I hear from Becca, okay?"

Not bothering to wait for a reply, Sam hung up the phone and scooted out of bed. He moved out to the hallway, where Michael and Daniel stood, both looking bleary-eyed and pale. Guess he wasn't the only one dealing with a rough hangover.

"You guys heard that too?"

Michael clenched his jaw and cocked his head to the side. "It sounded like a woman."

The screams started again, and Sam's stomach dropped to the floor. He'd heard that scream before, but the terror behind it was new. "Becca."

Sam ran for the stairs, Daniel and Michael hot on his heels, then flew down the steps. He turned the corner, ran down the hallway, and paused in the dining room to listen.

"It's coming from the basement," Daniel said.

Sam ran through the two kitchens and nearly tore the basement door off its hinges before scrambling down the basement stairs. The cell room. Good God, she was in the cell room. He lunged through the door to the room and froze in his tracks. As his eyes took in the scene, his heart thundered, and rage burned in his veins.

Becca was backed into the corner of a cell, screaming at the top of her lungs. Her blackened cheek was evidence that Amos had harmed her already. He stood in front of the cell, a sinister smile on his face.

"What are you doing?" Sam demanded.

"You broke the law, Sam," Amos said. "You told a human about us."

Sam flitted his gaze to Becca. She had stopped screaming. Her chest heaved as she took in terrified breaths, tears streaming down her face.

"She's no threat to us," Sam ground out.

"Of course not," Amos said. "Now that she's contained." Amos turned toward Becca. "She'll make a suitable mother as we grow our pack."

Cold dread settled into Sam's stomach. No. He couldn't be thinking of...

"Sam?" Becca's desperate voice tore at him. "Please, help me, Sam."

"You've chosen well, Sam," Amos said. "She's smart and attractive. She'll give me good offspring."

Every muscle in Sam's body tensed, and he clenched his fists. Becca desperately tried to back farther away from Amos. Something snapped inside him, and a feral growl rumbled in his throat. "Get away from her, Amos."

Amos turned toward Sam. When he studied Sam's features, Amos's eyes glowed yellow. "Are you challenging me, Sam?"

"You bet your ass I'm challenging you." Sam

sprang forward, morphing in midair, and landed on four giant wolf paws. With his teeth bared, he inched across the floor and growled.

Daniel and Michael must have changed as well, because Michael's excited bark of approval urged Sam on. Amos took a step away from the cell then shifted into his sleek black form. He crept forward, and they circled each other slowly.

Hiccupped sobs to Sam's right made him pause. Becca must have been freaking out. He swung his gaze away from Amos and stepped toward the cell. As he approached, he assessed her, making sure she was okay. She sobbed and backed away from him as he drew near. He smelled her terror, and it ripped a hole in him.

Her wide, frantic eyes scanned his body. His *wolf* body. Slowly, the terror in her eyes gave way to something else. Her posture relaxed. On a soft exhalation, she whispered his name. "Sam?"

He took another step toward her, hope squeezing his chest. *Please, let her accept me. Please.*

She leaned forward as though ready to come closer, then her face twisted into fear again. She pointed behind Sam and screeched, "Sam! Look out!"

Pain seared through the back of Sam's shoulder as sharp teeth tore into his flesh, and he let out a sharp yelp. He flipped around to his back, taking Amos with him, and pulled with just enough momentum to roll Amos onto his back so that Sam landed on top of him. Amos threw his head back, and Sam lunged forward to bite the alpha's throat.

Amos blocked Sam's shot with his snout, biting at Sam's face and neck. Sam ducked away from his shots, but he lost his footing and stumbled. They tussled on the floor, rolling in the dirt. Sam was quick, but Amos was strong, and years of experience had him anticipating Sam's moves.

Growing frustrated, Sam lunged at him head-on. Amos dodged out of the way then plowed into Sam, forcing him against the bars of the cell. As Sam's head was pinned toward the ground, he caught sight of Becca's tearful, anxious face.

"Sam, no! Please! Sam!" She reached out a hand. "Don't kill him, Amos. Please!"

From behind Sam came the yips and barks of Daniel and Michael. If he lost, they lost. Becca would die, and his pack would be forced to follow Amos. He couldn't let that happen.

Pushing as hard as he could, he threw Amos off his back and spun just as Amos lunged at him again. Sam went low, lunging straight for Amos's throat. He grabbed hold and locked his jaws, feeling the sticky wetness of Amos's blood between his teeth and sliding down his tongue to the back of his throat. Rage clouded Sam's brain, and all he wanted to do was drain the life from the alpha. The monster.

Loosening his jaw, Sam forced his rage down. He flung Amos to the side, and the alpha's limp body flopped to the floor.

Heaving, Sam limped forward. Amos gave rattling breaths. As Sam neared, Amos raised his head. Blood pooled beneath him.

"Do you yield?" Sam bared his teeth.

Amos's wolf growl gurgled as blood pulsed from his throat and bubbled from his mouth. The sound mingled with his projected laugh. *"Do you think this is over, pup? Do you think killing me will keep your girlfriend or your pack safe from the big, bad werewolf world? Your father was weak. He didn't prepare you for how it really is. The Council will never succeed in erasing our past. It's who we are. No matter how much you don't like it, there are more of us than there are of you.*"

Sam snapped at Amos and growled again. "*More of who?*"

"*Us, pup. The werewolf population you youngsters are trying to erase. You can't get rid of us. Tradition will always live on. Make your little surrogate agencies and try to change laws, but in a true werewolf's eyes, your little girlfriend will never be more than breeding stock.*"

Sam gave a low, menacing bark. The anger he had tried to keep contained moments ago flared to life. "*Yield.*"

Shakily, Amos lifted his head and stared into Sam's face. "*Never.*"

A part of Sam—the primal part of him that craved the kill—cheered as he once again went for Amos's throat. Biting down hard, he felt Amos's windpipe crush, and he shook his head, ripping the life from the former alpha.

He released his hold and stepped back, raising his head and letting out a long, low howl.

Behind Sam, Michael and Daniel howled with him, accepting him as the new alpha.

THIRTY-EIGHT

SAM

A chorus of howls echoed off the basement walls as Michael and Daniel bayed at their new alpha. Sam turned to them and howled with them, accepting their encouragement. They nipped and tackled each other, and Sam delighted at the lighthearted play that had been missing from their pack for almost two years.

As they danced in a circle around him, he momentarily forgot the human in the room. Then her smell hit him, and reality slammed back into him.

Sam peered into the cell where Becca was still huddled on the floor. Still terrified. Still hurt.

"Get Amos out of here before his body shifts back to human form."

"Whatever you say, alpha*!"* Michael yipped, hopping.

Daniel and Michael used their teeth to drag Amos's body out of the cell room and into the main room of the basement, out of Becca's view. The shift typically happened a few minutes after death. Becca didn't need to see Amos's mangled human body, not on top of everything else she'd seen.

He followed them out to the main room and

shifted. Michael and Daniel changed to human form as well.

"After he shifts, burn his body and scatter his bones." Sam eyed Amos. "I'm going to take care of Becca, then I'll talk to the Council."

On the floor, the large mass of black fur slowly morphed into Amos's human body. His throat was torn to shreds, and his eyes stared vacantly at the ceiling.

Sam felt no remorse or sadness. Amos had brought nothing but misery everywhere he went. The world was a better place without him. Sam had done the best thing he could for his pack by getting rid of Amos. He should have done it long ago.

Was that cold? Maybe. But as he looked at Michael and Daniel, he didn't care. His job was to keep them and Lucas and Roger safe. They were his pack. His responsibility. He would protect them at all costs.

Michael and Daniel started hauling Amos's body up the stairs, out of the basement, and Sam turned toward the shelves of boxes where the pack stored all their old things. At least a few boxes had old clothes mixed in. He found a pair of sweatpants and pulled them on.

Taking a deep breath, he rushed back into the cell room. He paused in front of the cell where Becca still sat on the floor. Her normally tan features had paled, and she looked like she was going to be sick. Tear tracks and smeared makeup covered her face, and a large black bruise made the side of her face swell. She hugged her knees tightly to her chest, and her hands shook vigorously.

Sam quickly went to work on the lock, and it opened with a click. The fear didn't leave Becca's eyes when they flicked in his direction. She didn't look relieved to see him. He missed the way her eyes used to light up when she saw him. Would they ever light up like that again?

He stepped toward her. She tensed, and her eyes widened. He froze. Holding his hands out in front of him, he slowly crouched to her level. She watched him closely as he inched toward her.

"Becca?"

"Sam?" Her voice wavered. Her eyes darted to his shoulder. "You're hurt."

Relief flooded through him. God, he'd been so afraid she'd checked out. "I'm okay."

A tear dripped down her cheek. "W-What? Do you, like, heal fast or something?"

Confusion clouded his brain for a moment before he realized she was thinking about werewolves in movies. He chuckled. "No. I don't heal fast. This will hurt for a while."

Another tear dripped down her cheek, but she didn't say anything.

"Can I come closer?" Sam spoke carefully. "Check to make sure you're okay?"

Becca blinked then nodded.

Sam scooted closer. He traced his fingers lightly over the bruise on her cheek, and anger sizzled inside him again.

"I-Is he g-gone? F-For good?"

Sam clenched his jaw. "You'll never see Amos again. I promise."

Becca nodded again. She dropped her knees then flung herself into Sam's arms. He fell backward onto his butt then wrapped his arms tightly around her. Her body shook as she hiccupped with sobs. Sam stroked her hair and whispered apologies into her ear.

THIRTY-NINE

ROSIE

Stuart straightened, a smile stretching across his face, his eyes bright with tears. He wasn't the frail man she'd last seen. This was the Stuart whose lap she fondly remembered sitting on years ago when she was just a little girl. She used to hang on his every word as she listened to him read from his journal. The Stuart she tried to cling to, before her memory was tainted by the image of his wolf form devouring the grandmother she never got the chance to know.

"So this is heaven?" His voice wavered, and he took another step forward. "I was pretty sure my number was up when Amos gave me a shove down the stairs."

"What?" Rosie gasped. After the words slammed into her, they made sense. She'd only been able to speak to her mother and father—both dead. "Stuart, are you dead?"

"I think I am." He stretched out his hands and studied them. "These aren't the wrinkled hands of an old man. If I'm not dead, I'm dreaming."

"Did you say Amos pushed you? Stuart—"

"Shh, that's not important." Stuart waved a hand.

"Amos will get his. Sam will see to that." He wrinkled his brow. "I don't know how I know that. I just do. You need to be more worried about Frank."

"Who?"

"He's even more evil than Amos. And he's angry. Amos betrayed him. Told him he'd bring him into the pack, then he didn't." Stuart clamped his mouth shut and scowled before he continued. "You'll find out soon enough. Just be careful."

"I don't understand." Rosie shook her head. Why did everything have to be a riddle?

"Just be careful, Rosie."

Rosie bit her lip. If Stuart was really dead, this might be her last chance to speak to him. For a long time, she hadn't been able to find it in herself to talk to him. Not really. She just couldn't get past what he'd done. She'd been flat-out rude to him. His pain had hit her every time she ignored him. She'd been so angry that she'd let him sit with that pain. That awful sorrow. Tears burned her eyes again.

"Stuart, I'm so sorry for the way that I acted."

"Oh, please, please don't do that." Stuart's eyes glistened as he shook his head. He furrowed his brow as though trying to find the right words. "I'm so sorry, dear. I've been trying to find the words to tell you how sorry I am. If you apologize to me, that just makes it harder, you know?"

A lump formed in Rosie's throat. She tried to swallow past it as the tears blurred the forest in front of her.

"If I could go back in time, I would erase it. I would erase it all." He averted his gaze, and a tear slipped down his cheek. "I'm not the same person I was back then, Rosie. And you are the reason for that."

Rosie flinched. "What do you mean?"

"You gave me a reason to be a better person. You gave me a reason to be a better man. I never..." He cleared his throat and took another step toward her. "I never gave any thought to what we were doing. Not at all. Until I knew you."

He let out a soft sob. The desire to take his pain and sorrow away drove her forward. She reached out to him, but he held out his hand. "No. I don't deserve your grace, girl. I don't deserve it. What I did was awful. What we did was awful. For generations, we killed. We murdered. It was wrong. It needs to be set right.

"My nightmares are plagued by the night I helped kill your grandmother. Only it's different. Your grandmother isn't the one the pack is killing." Another sob wracked his body. "It's you. Over and over again, I keep seeing your terrified face. You're in agony as you're torn to bits. I can't stand that I took part in that. I can't stand that I did that to another person."

Stuart sobbed again. Unable to hold back any longer, Rosie lunged forward and wrapped her arms around him. She hugged him close and let her calming energy seep into him. The quivering of his muscles eased, and he wrapped her in a tight embrace.

"I love you so much, dear girl." Stuart pulled away and looked into Rosie's eyes. A smile formed on his lips. "We all love you. We've missed you. It's time for you to go home."

"I can't go home." Rosie shook her head. "They want me to do things I can't do—"

"Stop, dear. You just keep being you. Do you see what you've done to me? If you can convince grumpy old Stuart to change his ways, there's hope for almost anyone."

"*Almost* anyone." Rosie frowned.

"There will always be those who resist change," Stuart said. "You can't worry about them. Concentrate on those who will listen. And there are so many who will."

Chewing on her lower lip, Rosie let her gaze wander around the forest. "How do I go home? I've been trying for days. It's no use."

As if to prove her wrong, the trees suddenly cleared away, and Hart House came into view. The freshly mowed lawn called to her. The garden...the trees...

"How..." Rosie couldn't form a sentence.

"Go home, Rosie." Stuart patted her shoulder gently. "They've been waiting for you."

"You're telling me someone punched you on the boardwalk?" A seething, red-faced Charlie ground his teeth as he grilled Becca for the tenth time that day. "And you didn't call the police?"

She'd had to think up the lie quickly when she finally showed up to work several hours late for her shift. Sam had tried to talk her into telling her father she couldn't come in, but she had to get away from Hart House and back to something normal. What had happened overnight was just too surreal.

Seeing Sam turn into a wolf had been terrifying at first. Then as she watched him, something about him as a wolf still seemed so *Sam*. How, she couldn't say, but even as a wolf, he was still her Sam, the Sam she knew and loved. She didn't have time to let that truly sink in before the fighting started.

When she thought Amos was going to kill Sam, she had been truly horrified. At that moment, she knew she couldn't live without him. Whether he was a human or a wolf, she needed him.

She'd covered her eyes when Sam went for Amos's throat, not wanting to see all that blood.

When it was all over, and Sam was human again,

he had gotten her out of that horrible cell and upstairs to the main living area. He held her and let her cry on him for a long time. When the tears were finally gone, they had some breakfast and talked.

They talked *a lot*.

So many questions still raced through her head, but she tried to push it all down and concentrate on just one thing. She loved Sam Hart. He came with heavier, freakier baggage than she could ever have dreamed, but she would take it on. She prayed that now that Amos was out of the way, the real danger had passed.

"It was dark, Dad." Becca rolled her eyes as she punched in the order for table seven. "I was scared and wanted to get home. As soon as I did, I just wanted to forget all about it."

"Well, you're going to talk to the sheriff today," Charlie grumbled. "I called Craig and told him about it. He's coming by this afternoon to take a statement."

"Dad, I can't tell him anything," Becca whined. "I didn't see the guy. I told you. I was out for a walk, he came up behind me, and pow!" Becca smacked her fist into her other palm.

"Why the hell would someone do something like that?" Charlie scratched his head. "Let me take a look at that bruise again."

Becca waved her father off as he leaned in to inspect the bruise. "Dad, you've looked at it a dozen times already. It hasn't changed. It was probably some drunk."

"Well, no more walking alone at night for you, young lady." Charlie put his hands on his hips. "And I'm getting you some mace to carry in your purse."

"Really?"

"Yes, really!" Charlie screeched. "I can't believe

you're not taking this more seriously. What did Sam say?"

Becca bit her lip as she watched Sam approach.

"I said as soon as I find out who hurt her, I'll rip him to shreds." As Sam spoke, he pulled Becca into a hug then kissed the top of her head.

Becca smiled. Sam wasn't exaggerating.

"You keep a close eye on our girl, Sam," Charlie said.

"Always."

"Go ahead and take a break." Charlie motioned toward the back of the restaurant. "I can cover your tables."

"You sure?"

"Yeah, I got it."

Sam took Becca's hand, and they moved to a booth in the corner of the restaurant. After they sat, he looked at her carefully.

"How you holding up?"

"I'm... letting things sink in." It was the best she could do. "How's your shoulder?"

"It'll be okay."

"Did you have your talk with your Council people?"

Sam laughed. "Yeah. They recognized me as the new alpha."

"Alpha." Becca tested the word on her tongue. "It sounds so official. So powerful. So..."

"Sexy?" Sam raised an eyebrow and cracked a smile.

Becca's cheeks heated. "Don't let it go to your head."

Sam's phone buzzed, and he squeezed her hand before he pulled it out of his pocket. His brow creased in concern when he looked at the screen then answered. "Clara?"

Becca straightened in her seat. Rosie's grandmother would only be calling with news of Rosie. Dread filled her stomach.

No. Please, no.

Sam's face paled, his jaw dropped, and Becca's stomach flipped. Tears stung her eyes, and she covered her mouth with her hands, shaking her head.

"Thanks, Clara. I'll be right there." Sam disconnected the call and met Becca's eyes. She almost didn't hear the whispered words she wasn't expecting. "She's awake. Rosie's awake."

The Hanks Hollow Series Continues…

Moon Over Hanks Hollow

Witch in a Wolf Den

When Witches Wake

THANK YOU!

Dear Reader,

THANK YOU for reading *Lost in Hanks Hollow*! These characters have become such a big part of my world, and I really hope you enjoyed meeting them. If you liked the story, please consider leaving a review on <u>Amazon</u> or <u>Goodreads</u>. Reviews and ratings help me so much, and I would be so grateful for the support!

For updates, follow me on Facebook, TikTok, or Instagram, and be sure to sign up for my newsletter!

https://linktr.ee/rachellekampen
https://www.facebook.com/rachellekampen
https://www.tiktok.com/@rachellekampen
https://www.instagram.com/rachellekampen/

ABOUT THE AUTHOR

Rachelle Kampen grew up on a farm in southern Wisconsin with three brothers and two sisters. In a rural setting with no cable television or internet, options for things to do were limited, so she read—a lot.

Though she's been writing stories from the time she learned to pen a sentence, she didn't take the leap into publishing until she started writing the Hanks Hollow series. The beloved characters and unique world of Hanks Hollow unite some of Wisconsin's fun quirks with a magical paranormal adventure.

She lives outside Madison, Wisconsin with her husband, daughter, two dogs, and two cats. Even now, with cable and internet at her fingertips, she loves a good book to pass the time.

You can find author Rachelle Kampen at:
https://linktr.ee/rachellekampen
https://www.facebook.com/rachellekampen
https://www.tiktok.com/@rachellekampen
https://www.instagram.com/rachellekampen/